A MOUNTAIN MAN'S
Redemption

Christi Corbett

A MOUNTAIN MAN'S
Redemption

CHRISTI CORBETT

A Mountain Man's Redemption
Copyright © 2015 by Christi Corbett

Published in the United States of America

Corbett, Christi
A Mountain Man's Redemption; novel/Christi Corbett
ISBN-10: 1518630243
ISBN-13: 978-1518630248

Cover Design by Roseanna White Designs
Cover Image from Shutterstock.com

Edited by Nia Shay

PRINTED IN THE UNITED STATES OF AMERICA

Dedicated to my Brother-in-Law

Darrel Philip Corbett

ACKNOWLEDGEMENTS

Christi's Sincere Thanks To...

My husband, Dalen Corbett, for his unwavering and overwhelming support of my writing career.

My twins, who let me borrow their GI Joes and Barbies so I can "act out" each movement of my fight scenes for accuracy.

Margo Kelly, my long-time critique partner, for pointing out magic gloves, disappearing snow, and for all her encouragement, advice, and pep talks over the past few years.

My Beta Readers: Tracy Smith, Michelle Naquin, Betty Christopherson, Jenny Bloom, Alyssa Morse, Barbara Brutschy, and Heather Trenk. Thank you all for taking time out of your busy schedules to read an early version of this book.

Nia Shay, for catching my numerous verb tense and hyphen mistakes, patiently explaining the difference between further and farther (again!), and being an all-around awesome editor.

Lou Klein, for generously allowing me to use his physical likeness for Philip's character, and for his input on Freddy's characteristics.

Scott Curry, for generously sharing his vast knowledge on fur trapping.

David Erickson, for advice about head and shoulder injuries, and for input on how guys fight.

Daniel Kallio, for his ideas about how to end the book.

Larry Chura, for clarifying gun options of the 19th century.

Matt Brode, Chief Meteorologist at KVOA, for his advice about snow and Montana winters.

Along the Way Home Announcers, for all their support and encouragement, as well as their generous input on cover art, back cover copy, and character names.

Staff of the Fern Ridge Library, for their help with research, and for giving me a quiet place to let my imagination run wild.

Ridge Writers, for offering endless input and advice about storylines and word choice.

And, as always, to Stephanie Taylor, for saying "Yes" when so many others said "No".

Chapter One
Urgency

Saturday, December 18, 1886

Philip Grant kicked dirt over last night's coals, turned west, and started walking. Now that he was trudging along the tree-covered hillsides on two legs instead of riding on four, he'd make ten miles by sunset. Twelve if he was lucky.

It figured his best friend and sole companion for the past eighteen years—his horse—would die while he was on his way to turn in his final bundle of furs and hang up his traps for good.

A staggering and ill-timed loss.

He had only ten days to get to Fort Matiley before it closed, and the hundred-pound bundle of furs burdening his back wasn't getting any lighter. Neither were his supply pack, bedroll, or meager amount of food and cooking utensils. Eighty miles of the most rugged mountain peaks in the Montana Territory stood between Philip and his retirement from a career he'd never wanted.

Habit brought his hands skimming along the leather belt around his waist, checking that his knife sheath and hatchet were tucked tight against his torso. Satisfied of their presence, his fingertips wandered to the powder horn swinging freely beside his left leg, his revolver in its leather holster hanging along his right leg, and then to the deerskin possibles bag slung across his chest.

He'd spent nearly two decades living on the move, and learned early on to seek constant reassurances of his possessions rather than waste time backtracking to find what he'd left behind.

Philip ducked under a low-hanging pine tree branch and grabbed a handful of small cones off the ground. They made for quick fire starters and he was eager to replenish his dwindling supply. Tucking the sticky bounty inside his coat pocket, he continued on.

During the first few miles of the day he kept his pace slow, unwilling to push his protesting muscles too hard against the early morning chill, but by the time the sun hung over the mountaintops he'd long since lengthened his stride.

Today he was crossing bare ground, but tomorrow

promised a different view—snow. Pain and stiffness in his elbow foretold of at least an inch later that night. Years ago he'd discovered his joints to be more reliable than any barometer he could have bartered his furs for at the trading posts.

Philip sidestepped a slight depression in the needle-covered forest floor, ever alert to the mirage of solid footing created by critters who covered their nests with branches and leaves to fool their predators. Walking through a cluster of ferns, he brushed his fingertips through the jagged blades and enjoyed the soft rustles of the silky fronds settling again after he'd passed.

Solitary life was rife with small pleasures if one knew where to look.

However, he was getting on in age—forty-eight. Too old to be traipsing about the woods and weather for months on end. His back ached from years of carrying furs and outdoor living, and he was eager to put all the wages he'd saved toward a more permanent arrangement. A cabin. Where he could put in some serious front-sittin' hours. On a porch. With his rump resting in a rocking chair and his fingers wrapped around a mug of tea.

While he'd miss the independence that came with being a free trapper—no work schedule, no boundaries, and above all, no one to report to beside himself— he was eagerly looking forward to what he *wouldn't* be doing.

No more spending hours wading along frigid rivers, his fingers fumbling to set steel traps that refused to stay in place. No more fighting to stay upright against currents that appeared calm for the first few steps, but turned swift and hungry once it was too late for man or beast to change course. No more waiting in a cold rain for his empty traps to snatch an inattentive beaver that civilization had long since deemed undesirable. Silk was the latest preference back east and abroad, and had been since before he'd taken a steamboat to Fort Benton.

Abandoning the life of a mountain man would allow his eyes to drift closed whenever he felt like it, instead of always on the alert to danger. Savages—of the two or four-legged variety—killed fur trappers. He had no desire to die in the woods alone, his body withering into oblivion beside a nameless stream. He'd rather die sitting before a roaring fire, surrounded by log walls and a weatherproof roof, having just eaten his fill of a good meal.

He was eager to live out the rest of his life in soft comfort, though he held no hope of attracting soft company. After all, what woman would want him once she learned why he'd abandoned the life he'd once known to live as a fur trapper?

A high-pitched screech sounded from the next hillside.

Philip lumbered toward a group of shrubs, ducked below their tops, and shrugged free from his furs and supply pack. He'd been so busy with his woolgathering he'd not only lost track of the time, he'd neglected the one thing that had kept him alive all these years—awareness.

Poised in a crouch that allowed him to either shift his weight or spin upon the balls of his feet to inspect his surroundings, he ran through the litany of animals or birds potentially responsible for what he'd heard. His stomach soured as all options led to nothing. Had a human made that noise?

Though no unusual sounds again filled the air, he slowly slid his knife from the sheath tied to his belt. Being prepared and anticipating danger always triumphed over relaxed contentment.

For the next several minutes he watched and listened. Nothing appeared out of place. The sky was dotted with swollen, graying clouds while the endless treetops swayed against the inevitable wind gusts. A murder of crows had taken respite throughout the branches of a fir tree and were squawking among themselves either about a territory war or upcoming departure plans for warmer land. Nothing unusual, yet nothing explained away what he'd heard. Or rather, what he thought he'd heard.

Philip ultimately convinced himself he'd fallen victim to trusting his aging ears a mite too much. Again.

Freddy wouldn't have tolerated such foolishness.

Over the past five years he'd trusted in and depended upon his horse's hearing more than his own, and he'd kept vigilant watch over the shifting positions of those long black ears. Ears that had never failed to give an early warning of approaching danger, nor had they ever turned away after Philip muttered concerns or confessions. Eyes that, while rarely judgmental, never failed to narrow when his companion was about to do something remarkably inept—which had happened countless times during Philip's first year of being a trapper.

Freddy's eyes would have certainly been narrowed now, begrudging being kept idle while Philip scouted the source of an imagined noise.

Resenting the amount of time he'd just wasted in needlessly playing lookout, Philip rose from the security of the shrubs. He ran his fingers from his forehead to the center of the back of his head, gathering and smoothing the top half of his shoulder-length black waves into a ponytail, then securing it tight with a thin strip of leather. As always, he allowed the bottom half to hang free. Once his furs and supply pack were settled again on his shoulders, he headed toward the next hill between him and Fort Matiley.

Minutes later he stood at the crest of that hill, staring in disbelief at what lay below.

Chapter Two
The Quilt

The navy patchwork quilt lying in a crumpled heap was completely out of place.

People who lived in houses used quilts. Civilized folks who only needed a few layers of cloth to keep away a chill when their fire died down while they slept. Anyone who'd spent more than a week traveling across the Montana Territory understood furs were better for warmth, and their hide offered unrivaled protection against the harsh, unpredictable weather.

With his muscles quivering and burning from the strain of remaining motionless, Philip studied the quilt again. Perhaps a traveler had brought it along, then discarded it when they'd become wise to its value? Judging by the condition—filthy would be a generous term—abandonment was a strong possibility. He certainly agreed with the decision. Several ragged patchwork squares flapped freely against the ever-present gusts of wind.

Philip's eyes narrowed when he realized the squares weren't the only things moving. Something alive was wrapped inside that quilt!

Shrugging free from his furs and supply pack, he moved closer.

Chapter Three
An Unlikely Discovery

The quilt—rather, whatever was in the quilt—moved three times over the next half-hour. From his new position—kneeling behind a fallen tree trunk about twenty yards downwind—Philip stroked his beard until it formed a point nearly four inches past his chin and analyzed his options.

Part of him wanted to grab his furs and go. He might be wasting sunlight and time—a precious commodity considering his looming deadline—for nothing more than a dying deer that had gotten itself tangled in a long-abandoned quilt.

The lump moved again.

Another fifteen watchful minutes passed, during which Philip's inner timekeeper worked itself into a seconds-tracking frenzy.

He could just end this odd standoff altogether. Fling aside an edge of the quilt and shoot whatever animal had the misfortune to find itself twisted within. Not to add any more pelts or skins to his bundle—already too heavy—but to finally move on, content with the knowledge he'd put a suffering animal out of its misery.

A clean conscious was more valuable than time saved.

His right hand stealthily palmed, then withdrew his knife by the twine-covered handle. No sense wasting a bullet when a precise slice with a blade would do the job. Striving for silence, he began to rise.

His body had other priorities. He held back a groan as blood rushed through stretching muscles. By the time he'd gotten his feet flat on the ground, his heartbeat pounded in his ears. His knees and back vehemently protested any movement—clicks and pops echoed with each inch he straightened. Then, the second he was fully upright, he pitched forward. It took three stumbling steps to regain his balance.

Growing old humbled a man like little else.

He took another step, gritting his teeth as tingling pain shot down his right thigh and ended at his toes, which had long since gone numb. He allowed himself a minute of respite, then got moving. Staying low, he sidestepped twenty paces to his left, stopping behind a pine tree. The trunk concealed only half his body, but it was better than open ground. Plus it allowed him a pushing off point. Tangling with a wild animal, no matter how small, required preparation and a head start.

Curling his right forearm around the tree, he leaned left and eyed the quilt, now less than fifteen yards away. After a few minutes, he frowned.

Nothing.

No movement. No noise. Nothing.

Philip shook his head in disgust. *Enough of this!* He'd wasted daylight and lost miles for nothing more than fabric flopping in the wind. Done with caution and eager to kick the quilt open, confirm nothing lay inside, and then be on his way again, he stepped from behind the trunk.

Three feet from the quilt he stumbled mid-step and his eyes went wide. He'd been so intent on figuring out what was inside the quilt he'd missed seeing what lay curled in the dirt along one end.

A long lock of blond hair.

Chapter Four
A Familiar Sound

Philip stowed his knife and peered into the folds of fabric surrounding the hair. He saw a glimpse of forehead and nothing more. Leaning closer did no good. Too dark inside. Uncertain what to do next, he settled for asking what he figured was the most pertinent.

"You all right in there?"

No reaction.

He tried again. "You awake?"

Something rustled beneath the quilt, near where he guessed the person's stomach to be. "I see you moving, so you might as well show yourself."

An animalistic screech of frustration—the same one he'd first heard from over the hillside—sounded from deep within the quilt. Seconds later, all went silent save for a faint, repetitive sound he couldn't quite place.

Until he could.

Philip sat back on his heels, struggling to banish the sudden rush of memories the noise had recalled. A noise that reminded him of the happiest, and then the most devastating time of his life. A noise he'd spent the last eighteen years trying to escape.

"Woman, if you can hear me, it's time to let me know." Sincerely hoping for an answer and dreading what he'd find if he didn't, he leaned in until his lips were mere inches from the lock of hair. "I give you my word I won't hurt you."

Nothing.

He stared at the quilt, uncertain when to stop waiting and finally open it himself. And hope doing so wouldn't confirm his worst suspicions at what lay inside.

The soft, rhythmic noise continued.

Panic stole the air from Philip's lungs and the light from his eyes, forcing him to brace a steadying hand against the ground. Only when his breaths were strong and sure again did he trust himself enough to reach tentative fingers forward.

"I'm about to lift this quilt," he whispered, fearing what was inside couldn't reply. Fearing what was inside was fighting a losing battle too horrific to fathom.

Then, one raspy word changed everything. "Don't."

Chapter Five
Revealing All

A filthy fingertip emerged from the quilt, curled over the edge, and pulled it down low enough to reveal two bright blue eyes—one wide with fear and the other surrounded by swollen purple flesh.

"Hello," he said, taking care to keep his tone light, comforting.

"Hello," she whispered in muffled reply.

Lacking any idea of what to do next, Philip stayed silent and still. However, he allowed his gaze to roam about the area in a search for clues. He found two—darkened dirt less than a foot from her head confirmed a recent bout of vomiting, and a smear of dried blood on her forehead confirmed her left eye wasn't her sole injury.

"You cold?" he asked, trying to figure whether she

shook from cold or fear.

Her eyes never left his as she slowly shook her head. Fear it was.

"I won't hurt you." He repeated his earlier assertion in case she hadn't heard.

She replied—not with words, but by sliding the quilt lower.

Philip rewarded her show of trust with an encouraging smile. A smile he held, albeit stretched tighter, when he sighted crusted blood in her hair along her left temple. It didn't falter when he noticed the inch-long gash on her left cheekbone, nor did it waver after she pulled the quilt past her mouth and he saw the right side of her bottom lip was split and swollen.

No wonder she'd stayed silent.

But when she lowered the quilt yet again, revealing finger-width bruising across her neck, Philip couldn't hold up the reassuring farce any longer. He clapped a hand over his mouth to stifle a gasp at the long-ago familiar sights.

The center of the quilt moved again, and he took note of the round lump—her elbow or knee?—pushing against the fabric as if trying to break free.

"Do you want to come out of there?" he asked.

She shook her head.

He regretted the words even as he spoke them. What if she were unclothed? Hurt so badly she couldn't move? Or even worse, what he suspected lay beside her was true?

"Can you sit up?" he asked.

She shook her head in adamant refusal.

"Why not?"

With the wary desperation of someone who knows escape is impossible and there's no option but to surrender, she slowly raised the quilt.

A baby was curled against her chest.

Chapter Six
Dinner Guests

Philip sat back on his heels and let out a low whistle at the confirmation of his earlier assumption. At least it wasn't his most feared prediction, which would have led to him traipsing through the mountains, seeking out the father of a motherless baby.

The baby, startled at the sudden noise, turned from its nourishment and stared at him with eyes that matched its mother's.

Philip went motionless under the inquisitive gaze, wishing he'd bothered to comb his hair and beard that morning. Or at least that week. The child might think him a wolf or grizzly given how wild he'd let himself go. Daily grooming and weekly cleaning of his clothes and body had fallen by the wayside since Freddy died.

Philip strived for something to show both the baby

and mother he was friendly, if not well washed. Knowing his teeth were all intact and relatively clean due to regular ministrations with his bone-handled toothbrush, he smiled.

Within seconds, the baby's whimpers turned to wails.

Memories swarmed and Philip reached out an instinctive hand, intending to calm. The action had the opposite effect—the woman curled her arm around the child and shrank from his reach, protective of everything she'd just willingly revealed.

"Sorry," he murmured, lowering his hand back to his side, embarrassed and saddened at how his clumsy attempt of recreating how he'd handled a fretful child from his past had reduced her to fearful shudders.

"I'm going fetch my furs and supplies." He motioned toward the hillside where he'd abandoned his packs when he'd caught sight of the quilt and sent his day awry. "Then I'll come back and make a fire." Sighting the hunger in her eyes, he added, "Probably make some food too. You and your young'un are welcome to share both."

Her gaze darted from the knife stowed in his belt to the revolver at his side and then settled on his eyes. He remained silent and steadfast, understanding her need to judge his character even though she was powerless to protect herself if his intentions were cruel.

Finally she nodded her agreement.

Working with an efficiency born of years of practice, Philip searched for pine needles and cones, moss, and dry twigs. He returned and piled what he'd found a few feet from where the woman lay beneath her quilt, presumably still nursing the baby.

Another trip out yielded an armload of burnable branches. Deferring to his newfound guests' obvious sensitivity to loud noises and sudden movements, he took care to break the fuel down into manageable lengths far away from the makeshift camp. Upon his return, he found the woman sitting up within the folds of the quilt and the baby cradled in her arms. While she warily watched his every move, her child ignored his presence, favoring instead to chew mightily on what was clutched in its hand—a green piece of cloth no bigger than a canteen.

"Which kind you got there?" Philip asked, digging through his pack in search of his flint.

Her creased brow and cocked head showed her confusion at his question.

He nodded to the baby. "Girl or a boy?"

Instantly, her features changed from tentative to proud. "Boy." Her voice was surprisingly coarse given her petite frame and young age. Philip glanced again at the bruising on her neck and deemed it the cause of her husky tone. Poor girl.

Having nothing else to say at the moment, he toed aside the thick layer of needles until he reached bare ground. He then dug his right heel into the dirt and walked a backward circle. Once the ring was complete he started a fire within its confines, then emptied his pack of all he'd need to make pemmican mash—a serving spoon and a pot. Thankfully a creek ran strong less than a quarter-mile away. With his canteen strap across his palm, he rose, then looked to the woman.

"Going for water. Back soon."

She nodded her reply, then bowed her head to focus on her son.

Philip glanced around camp. He had no qualms about leaving his furs behind. The woman was frail, carrying a child, and there was nowhere for her to run to even if she could lift them. While he'd lost count after forty, he estimated it contained nearly sixty made beavers. A few rabbits and foxes were in there too. His possibles bag, his journal with his hard-earned wages hidden within, and his weapons were another thing entirely. After gathering everything he couldn't replace and tucking it into his belt, he headed out.

True to his word, he was back and setting the pot atop the flames within fifteen minutes. Philip pulled the bag of pemmican from his pack, cut off his usual amount and tossed it in the pot, then glanced at the woman and boy. Both watched him with hunger in their eyes. Wordlessly, he added another portion to the pot.

He motioned to the boy. "He old enough to eat real food?"

She nodded, then gave him a grateful smile.

Philip busied himself over the fire, pouring water into the pot until it covered the pemmican, then waited for several minutes. Once the lumps were warm and soft, he smashed them with the back of the spoon, then slid a lid over the fragrant, bubbling mixture. After setting the spoon on a flat rock, he flipped open an outer flap on his pack and brought out a paper bag.

"Food will be ready in about twenty minutes, but I've got something that will help in the meantime." He removed a thick piece of jerky from the bag. Figuring the boy was old enough to gnaw on his own piece, he tore the meat in two and handed both to the woman. A tin cup filled with water soon followed.

"Thank you," she whispered, inching closer to the fire.

Satisfied he'd done what he could to sate their immediate concerns, he sat back against his furs, stretched out his legs, and crossed them at the ankle. Once he'd made himself comfortable, he proceeded to study his guests.

Chapter Seven
Evaluations

The matted blood in the woman's hairline near her temple concerned Philip the most. It indicated a hard hit to the head—either by fall or fist—and foretold of lasting issues with vision, balance, and concentration. Not to mention additional problems from the blood loss. Her shirt bore the telltale stain from the left shoulder all the way to the end of her sleeve. The swollen flesh around her left eye and the cut on her cheekbone would heal given time and proper care.

Proper care included taking nourishment, and judging by the trouble her busted lip was giving her while she bit jerky and sipped water, eating was difficult. Not that she was able to keep it down—the dirt beside her showed another spreading stain. He studied it, then concluded she'd vomited again while he'd been out gathering wood or water. It didn't bode well for her if it was the result of the simple action of sitting up.

She caught him staring and lowered her head, then further attempted to conceal her injuries by pulling her hair over the left side of her face and curling it along the front of her neck. A heartbreakingly familiar action, and one that did no good since he'd already seen everything she was now trying to hide.

Or had he?

What if his earlier thoughts were correct and she was suffering from further injuries? Bruised organs? Broken bones? Or another type of problem entirely—lack of pants?

As he pondered what was rapidly becoming an overwhelming amount of things to ponder upon, the boy let out a squeal and waved his left hand triumphantly in the air, jerky clutched between his chubby fingers.

By all appearances, he seemed free from any injuries like those that plagued his mother. Philip noted that the boy was older than he'd first thought. At least a year, perhaps a month or two more. Too young to walk or talk much, and he'd still be a burden with his needs—consistent amounts of food, sleep, and playtime. At the same time, old enough to cause trouble by getting into what he shouldn't, or crawling out of sight the moment a watchful eye wavered.

As if sensing Philip's evaluation of him, the boy

stopped fidgeting in his mother's arms, his jerky forgotten for the moment in favor of staring at the man who'd given it to him. Unaccustomed to such direct scrutiny, especially the unabashed attention that only a child could give, he resisted the urge to smooth a hand over his beard and hair.

The boy quickly tired of Philip, and of holding still. Little squirms soon turned into back-arching attempts to wiggle free from his mother's grasp until he fell hard against her on his right side, causing his mother to cringe and the boy to wail.

Seeing how she was quick to lower her lips to his head and murmur words of comfort, all while curling her arms around him and swaying a consistent rhythm, Philip concluded her to be a protective, if not competent, mother to the boy. After all, what mother in her right mind would be in the middle of a forest that was rife with wild animals and even wilder men?

Once the boy had quieted again, Philip filled his sole plate with a hearty serving of mash, stuck a fork in the middle of the pile, and handed it to the woman.

"Thank you," she said. Then, holding what he'd given far from the reach of the boy's eager fingers, she bowed her head and closed her eyes.

Praying.

Philip, with the serving spoon halfway between the pot and his lips, halted in midair, more out of courtesy than agreement. When she was finished, he started eating directly from the pot, taking extra care not to spill. He refused to slurp from his shirtfront or pick morsels from his beard in front of his guests.

Three bites in he glanced across the fire to see their progress. To his stunned disbelief, the plate was already empty and the boy was bent over, licking it clean. Philip swallowed what he held in his mouth, and felt it drop into his rapidly souring stomach. He couldn't in good conscious take another bite.

Tilting the pot, he scraped what remained into a clump. "I ate earlier so I'm full. Don't want this to go to waste, so hold out that plate."

Wordlessly, but with a look of intense gratitude, she leaned forward and did as directed.

Chapter Eight
Introductions and Lies

Philip wiped the cooking and serving dishes clean, then settled himself back against the bundle of furs again. He stared at her for a long time, waiting for her to speak. Unlike most women he'd known, this one seemed content with silence. Regardless, certain things needed to be worked over, so he might as well start it off. "You got a name?"

"Hannah." She cringed and put a fingertip to her swollen lip. "Hannah Dolt."

He looked to the boy, now playing a game with himself of putting the green cloth on his head and then pulling it off again. "And him?"

"Clark." Hannah ran a loving hand across her son's wispy blond hair, smoothing it from his forehead. "Named after William Clark, the explorer. I wanted him to have the name of a great man who'd done great things. Unlike his father."

Philip took note of, but didn't pursue, her last statement. "How old is he?"

"His first birthday was the twenty-eighth of last month."

"How old are you?"

Her eyebrows furrowed and she stared into the treetops for nearly a minute. "Seventeen?" she finally answered, her tone reflecting her uncertainty. After another few seconds of contemplation she gave a decisive nod. "Yes, I'm seventeen."

Philip frowned, unsure if she was poorly educated in numbers or the head wound was playing havoc on her memory. "Do you know what year it is?"

"1886."

"How about the month?"

Her stare settled again on the treetops as she considered his question, but to his relief she answered correctly. "December."

"And the day?"

"This one I know." She clasped her hands together, and her eyes hinted of a growing inner confidence. "It's Friday."

"Close." Perhaps her home had no calendar or ability to track days of the year. "It's Saturday, December 18, 1886."

Normally he didn't keep such close watch over the date, but he was checking his own calendar every morning so he could know how long he had until the closure of Fort Matiley.

"Saturday?" Her eyes widened in surprise. "I've been here for a whole day?"

"Seems so," he said, again eyeing her temple. "Speaking of that, why are you out with no supplies?" he asked, waving his arm across the trees surrounding them on all sides. "With a baby?"

"We enjoy the silence."

Philip narrowed his eyes as he evaluated the obvious lie. This woman wasn't in the woods for solitude.

He nodded toward the quilt, then Clark. "You've got to know better than to be outside in the middle of December, with only a thin quilt to protect yourself and that baby."

She shrugged.

Unsatisfied with her cavalier attitude, he drove the point further. "Foolish of you to head out alone, and even more so to take along a young'un. Life in the woods often requires staying hidden. Can he follow simple commands? Most important, be quiet when told?"

"He's a good boy," she replied, her features taking on a hardness that hopefully reflected stubbornness below her soft surface. "And I have ways to keep him occupied when I need to."

"I don't doubt you can keep him busy. What I do doubt is the reason you say you're out here."

"I got lost." Her words came easy, but the crimson hue flooding her cheeks told of her untruth.

Philip bit the inside of his cheek, holding back a retort for fear of scaring her with his rising frustration. His stomach was tight with hunger and would be for the foreseeable future since he'd just handed over half his rations for the coming week. Even worse, he was sitting idle in the middle of the day—prime travel time. And she had the audacity to lie?

Oblivious to his irritation, she dug in further. "I only meant to take a quick walk," she said, then motioned to Clark, now drowsily snuggling the folds of the quilt. "I wanted to show him a squirrel. I took a few wrong turns and then—"

"There's nothing out here," he interrupted. "No homes, at least that I know of. No settlement. And certainly no town. The nearest town is over a mountain range, at least sixty miles away." Fed up with her evasiveness and lies, he asked again. "Why are you really out here?"

"Why are you out here?" she challenged in return.

"Not your concern." He gave her the same glare his wife used to say was so fierce it could send a lumberjack to his knees. It was long past time to address what they both had been dancing around, neither wanting to put it into words. "The forest ain't quiet and those marks on your face ain't from falling, so how 'bout you quit spouting lies and tell me what you're running from?"

Her chin trembled as tears spilled down her cheeks. "My husband's fists."

Chapter Nine
Testing her Fire

Philip gulped hard as a rush of hot bile rose in his throat. Only when his stomach had settled again did he trust himself to speak. "Your husband did that to you?"

"Yes."

Philip nodded to the boy, now fully asleep. "He know you're out here with his son?"

A series of useless motions—smoothing the wrinkles from her shirtsleeve, examining the dirt beneath her fingernails, and rearranging the section of quilt covering Clark—preceded the answer she reluctantly gave.

"No."

So she'd fled. He looked around, suddenly uneasy. Dealing with injuries while dragging a quilt and carrying a fussy, scared child made for a slow pace; she couldn't have gotten far from her home. Five miles at the most.

He rose to his feet and walked a wide circle around their camp, taking extra care to notice any signs of someone watching her aside from himself.

"What's out there?" she asked while he was still a good ten yards out. "Do you see something?"

He waved off her questions, and then put a finger against his lips to command her silence. Her immediate look of chagrin told him she'd realized her error. Minutes later, once he'd assured himself no one was lurking nearby, he returned to the fire.

The girl before him had been strong enough to escape, but did she have the inner fire to stay away? To stand up to those who would insist a woman was the property of her husband and therefore must capitulate and obey his every command? To shield herself and her boy from a husband determined to have both back at any cost?

He understood what she was doing for herself and her son, but others wouldn't. Judgmental looks and words whispered behind cupped palms didn't leave visible wounds like a hand raised in anger, but the sting was almost as cruel.

Philip ran a thumb and forefinger along his lips, then gave her a speculative look. "Some would say a boy needs his father. Some would say you're a coward, and you made a commitment before God and your family to honor your marriage through to the end."

"I had to leave! There's no way—"

A fit of coughing rendered her speechless, and putting her hand to her throat did nothing to relieve her raspy spasms. It seemed her sudden fury was no match for the damage her husband's choking fingers had left across her neck. It took half a cup of water and several minutes of testing swallows for her willingness to speak to return. And what she said when it did crushed Philip to his core.

"I'm sorry I got mad."

Philip held up his hand. "No need for an apology. I'm on your side."

"Then why…?" She trailed off in confusion.

"I wanted to see if you'd fight back, show your strength when challenged." He gave her a tender, reassuring smile. "You did just fine."

Chapter Ten
The Letter

Twilight settled in, bringing along its usual companions: chilly temperatures and the dwindling ability to see surroundings. Philip eyed the stack of sticks sitting beside the glowing coals. "I'd build up this fire, but if you're expectin' pursuit, the light will be a giveaway."

Hannah's lips pursed together in a bitter line and she shook her head. "The only thing William's ever pursued with any perseverance is the bottom of a bottle."

Satisfied but still leaving his revolver within reach, Philip tossed two more branches across the dwindling flames, then leaned back as a shower of sparks flew into the air. Once the fire settled, he met her gaze again.

"I don't have much, but you're welcome to whatever will help you and your boy get to where you're going."

Philip pulled his pack to his side, already cyphering on what he could leave with her and the boy. He could spare a few pelts to act as a barrier between the cold ground and her quilt, a full canteen, his flint in case she let a fire go out and needed to get it started again, and what remained of his stash of jerky, save for a single piece for himself.

Traveling the next eighty miles would be tough, but it was a sacrifice he'd gladly make to help out a woman and child in such obvious need.

With his spare canteen in hand, Philip paused as he realized he didn't know what to give her, because he didn't know what she had planned. Was she heading somewhere specific, or had she just fled without considering what to do next? Was she waiting out here for a few more hours, or maybe a day, for whoever she had hopefully arranged to get them and bring them to safety?

"What are you going to do now?" he asked. "Do you have somewhere to go?"

"My aunt's house."

"Where's that?"

"She's a wonderful woman. My mother's sister. She insists she's got plenty of room for me and Clark."

Philip let her ramble on, enjoying her excitement as she spoke about the new life she'd planned for herself. Seemed he was wrong about his earlier impression of her not being a woman who filled silence with chatter. She'd just needed to warm up to him first.

"She's a crafty, tenacious woman. Last month I got a knock at the door from one of her neighbors. He's a good neighbor, traveling all that way just to bring me a letter from my aunt."

Philip's curiosity rose upon hearing the phrase 'all that way', but he didn't interrupt.

"He'd waited around the side of the house until William left for the day, then he knocked on the door and gave me the letter." Her eyes went hard. "My aunt must have warned him about the kind of man my husband was, because he lit out again real fast. Wouldn't even stay for a cup of coffee and a chat."

Philip sensed the solitary nature of where she'd lived, combined with her husband's brutal nature, didn't allow for many lingering visitors.

"Anyway, I opened that letter up right quick, and found out my parents were dead. Barn caught fire, and they both died trying to free the livestock. House went up too. Everything's gone, and all that's left of my childhood was the family bible that my mother carried outside and then dropped in the garden on the way to the barn."

Her shoulders rose and fell as she let out a deep sigh.

"Inside the bible were letters I'd written to my parents. The first, pleading for them to reconsider their decision to make me marry William and to let me come home. The second, telling them of how he'd beaten me so bad I'd given birth to their grandson a month before his time. I again begged to come home. They never wrote me back."

Her voice cracked and she pressed her sleeve beneath her nose until her sniffles subsided.

"My aunt found the letters after the fire, and she sent me one in return. She had no idea, she'd been told by my parents all was well, and how happy I was in my marriage. All lies. She wrote how if I ever decided to leave William, that Clark and I were welcome in her home. Forever."

Clark waved his left arm in the air, then grabbed a lock of her hair and clutched it in his fist. She bent to kiss his forehead and while he was distracted, she gently untangled the blond strands from his fingers. Once she'd pushed her hair over her shoulder and out of his inquisitive reach, she looked to Philip again. "Her letter was a lifeline of hope."

Philip nodded understandingly. He didn't even know the woman, and he was overcome with admiration for how quickly she'd acted once she knew the truth of her niece's situation. "What does your uncle have to say about her plan?"

"My aunt is a widow. My uncle died two years after

they got married." The sleeve appeared again, this time wiping tears from her cheeks. "She never had children of her own, but she was more of a mother to me than my own. My parents were always busy, so I stayed with my aunt for long stretches of time. She taught me how to cook, sew, keep house, read…"

She clasped her hand over her mouth, stifling uncontrollable sobs. Philip sat, quiet and uncertain, his determination not to scare her overshadowing wanting to offer her comfort. He settled for holding out a handkerchief, which she accepted with a weak smile.

"She warned me about William. I was so caught up with him that I refused to listen. We got in a horrible fight, and less than a week later it was too late to tell her how wrong I'd been. I was married and moving on."

"Your aunt sounds like a wise, wonderful woman." *And a forgiving one.*

"She's all the family I have left now," Hannah said wistfully, then glanced down at the boy in her arms, now squirming for freedom. "Besides my boy."

While he appreciated her honesty, Philip was growing apprehensive about where her aunt lived. There was nothing but mountains to the west and desolate plains to the east, so where could she possibly be heading? Perhaps the aunt lived in a cabin nearby? If so, it had to be relatively new. He'd spent years traveling up and down, across and around these hills, and didn't recall recently hearing the telltale ringing of an ax or seeing freshly fallen trees. Though, given Hannah and Clark had come from somewhere close by too, he might have also missed her aunt's house.

"I have great memories of Christmas with her at her house. We'd spend the entire week in the kitchen, working together to make all kinds of sugary and savory treats for the Christmas Eve dinner at our church. Then, after reading from the bible about the birth of our savior, we'd snuggle in her bed and talk late into the night about anything and everything. On Christmas morning we'd drink crisp apple cider and eat warm cinnamon rolls, and open a few gifts. She always made me feel special and loved." Hannah's eyes were shining with excitement and anticipation. "I planned to surprise her for Christmas."

Philip gave her a skeptical look. "Seems the word 'planned' is a stretch." While he admired the courage it must have taken for her to leave, he hated the way she'd gone about it—unprepared.

"I know what you're thinking," she said.

His eyebrows rose with intrigue. "What am I thinking?"

"That my past mistakes are now putting my son at risk. That I've run off in the middle of winter with nothing more than what I could carry. That if I had a lick of sense I'd have planned better."

"You're right." Philip shrugged. "At first I thought everything you just said, and much more." He'd also thought how much he'd wished his own mother had been brave enough to do what Hannah had done—risk it all to escape a lifetime of beatings, or worse, for her and her boy. "But I also think you're the bravest woman I've ever met. You're doing right by yourself and your child, and that's what's most important."

"Are you a Godly man, Philip?"

Her question caught him off guard, but he had no reason to lie. "Not lately."

Hannah placed her palm across Clark's chest and leaned down to kiss the top of his head before settling her gaze on Philip once again. "Please," she whispered, "help us."

Chapter Eleven
Considerations

"What more do you need from me?" he asked, eyeing his supply pack for what else he could possibly provide.

"To take us to my aunt's house." She paused, her gaze unwavering yet unsure. "In Great Falls."

"Great Falls?" he stammered in disbelief. "Why, that's sixty miles away from here!"

"Seventy," she corrected, then straightened her spine as a newfound determination took hold. "And I need you to take us there."

Hoping he'd heard her wrong, he sought clarification. "You've known me less than two hours, and you're asking me to take you all the way to Great Falls?"

"Yes," she said, nodding.

Philip stared at her, amazed at both her audacity

and tenacity. "And you've brought along nothing by way of supplies—no food, no canteen, no bedroll."

"Correct," she said, nodding harder.

Letting out a long sigh, Philip rested his elbows on his knees and dug his fingers deep into his hair. Time was tight. If he wasn't standing in the doorway of Fort Matiley by December 28th, he'd be forced to bring his furs another two hundred miles farther west to the next trading post—already closed for the season—and wait until it reopened next spring. A huge setback and an outlandish risk, especially given the heavy snowfall and frigid temperatures guaranteed to hinder his progress.

Bringing her along to Fort Matiley would require her to cross countless rugged and rocky hillsides. No chance she'd be able to keep up the pace needed to make his ten day deadline. Besides, she'd never survive the return trek across the same mountains.

It had to be her way, not his.

Hannah mistook the reason behind his silence. "My parents, myself, and my aunt were some of the first residents of Great Falls, long before it had an official name. My aunt wrote that it's grown steadily since I left, and it's now a nice place to settle down and raise my boy."

"I agree," Philip replied.

Great Falls was a relatively new town in the Montana Territory. They'd only established a post office two years ago, and the previous year when he'd passed through he'd seen the beginnings of what a town needed to surpass a shantytown designation—a mill, lumber yard, bank, school, a newspaper, and an organized street layout. He'd also heard talk how the Great Northern Railway was considering setting rails through in the next year or two. The town was designed to thrive when the inevitable influx of people flocked to newfound civilization. It was a good town to raise a family, showed a lot of promise for withstanding growth, and had a solid future as a stronghold for the area.

It was also situated a hundred and fifty miles in the opposite direction of where he was headed.

Philip laced his fingers together across the back of his neck and stared at the woman who'd turned his day into chaos. The woman now waiting for his answer. He appreciated her understanding of his need to evaluate what she'd proposed, and how she wasn't trying to influence him with tears, guilt, or any of the other wily ways women had available to influence a man's decision.

"Hannah, the problem is simple—you need to go east, and my entire future depends upon me heading west." He threw up his hands in frustration. "Why should I abandon my plans for yours?"

Her nostrils flared and her eyes turned fierce. "Because if I stay out here my son and I will die, and if I go back my husband will kill me."

Chapter Twelve
Harsh Words

She was right, of course. No way would the man she'd described ever let his wife forget such a massive betrayal.

"Can you tell me what you're thinking?" Her voice was timid, yet hopeful.

"I'm thinking how I should have been five miles farther west right now." His left eye started to twitch and he pressed his fingertips into the spot just above his cheekbone. "I'm thinking how instead I'm sitting here, negotiating with myself on how to accept the demise of everything I've worked so hard to achieve."

"I know I'm asking a lot—"

"You have no idea what you're asking of me." He scrambled to his feet and snatched a branch from the pile he'd dropped beside the fire earlier. "Well, let me fill you in. You're asking me to sacrifice everything because you finally decided you'd had enough, and left without preparing for, or even considering, what you'd do five feet past the edge of your porch."

He meant to toss the branch in the middle of the fire, but the jagged end caught on his sleeve, sending it sideways into the air. Hannah flinched as it tumbled to a stop in the dirt before her, then she cowered into the quilt, bowing her head and curling her arms protectively around Clark, who immediately began to whimper.

"I'm sorry," Philip said, anxious to reassure. "I didn't mean to scare you. The stick slipped out of my hand. Momentum sent it to you, not anger."

She ignored him in favor of trying to calm her tearful son.

"I'm sorry," he repeated, disgusted with himself for allowing his frustration to creep into his earlier tone, and words. Her request was straightforward, stemmed from a solid reason, and it wasn't her fault it created a massive impact on his own life. "I've never hurt a woman or a child in my life, and I have no intention of starting now."

Hannah raised her head and met his gaze. Her eyes showed tentative forgiveness, but her arms remained tensed in readiness should he suddenly prove himself a liar. Meanwhile, Clark had no concerns aside from escaping his sudden confinement. After a brief struggle, he freed his left arm from both the quilt and his mother's grip. His right arm remained still. Awkwardly still.

Ashamed of his outburst, Philip spent the next few minutes laying out his bedroll in front of the fire, taking care to move slowly so as not to startle Hannah or the boy. While he worked, he berated himself.

He of all people should have known better. Judging by the seriousness and condition of her injuries, she'd been beaten to near death less than two days ago. He'd done little more than badger her for information, rant about how her boy needed a father, and then he'd thrown a stick at her. What was he thinking, being so rough? She was barely past being a child herself!

Once he finished smoothing the top blanket, he sat. Immediately his torso and shoulders collapsed forward, as if unable to bear the choice forced upon him. What he heard next only made things worse.

"I can pay you."

Chapter Thirteen
Offering Everything

Clutching Clark—who'd fallen asleep while Philip had laid out his bedroll—tight against her chest, she reached deep within the quilt, presumably into a pocket, and then pulled her hand out with a proud flourish. "I have money."

She extended her arm toward him and opened her fingers. Sitting on her palm were a few silver coins, an insultingly meager amount of money for what she was proposing.

"I want to pay you for tonight's dinner, the rest can hopefully go toward your services as a guide to Great Falls."

Philip mentally tallied her offering. Three dollars.

Instead of being offended, he was honored. She'd mentioned her husband's fondness for drink, which meant he was the type to spend extra money—or perhaps even money that should have gone to necessities like seeds and a plow—on the brave-maker in the brown bottle. It had probably taken her years to hide away those coins.

"Keep it," he said, brushing aside her offer with an insistent flick of his wrist.

She held her hand aloft, shaking it so the coins clinked together as if confident the noise would tempt, then persuade him into agreement.

"I'm not living out here because I need money," he said, cocking his head and allowing a chiding smile to cross his lips. His fur bundle contained nearly sixty made beavers, and each one would bring him nearly twice what she offered. Not to mention the payment he'd receive for the other pelts he'd collected.

Her brow furrowed. "Why would you be living in the mountains with no house or land if you don't need money?"

"I have my reasons." Two reasons, actually. One had been small, innocent. The other had been capable of something he'd never imagined possible.

Clark stirred, likely from the continued clinking of the coins in Hannah's palm. Philip went motionless, as did Hannah, in the unspoken bond of adults who want a woken child to drift off again. The boy's eyelids slowly closed, then snapped open. The corners of his lips curled into a grin and despite his mother's fervent crooning and weary sighs, he struggled to sit up.

Philip chuckled as the boy began waving at him across the fire. After a sympathetic glance to Hannah, Philip wiggled his own fingers in reply. Hannah tolerated their impish antics for a few minutes, then, with the coins on her palm, she again extended her arm toward Philip as if to remind him of her unresolved proposition.

"Please. It's all I have to give." Her voice and eyes lowered. "Take it. I can't make it without your help and it's worth nothing to Clark if I'm dead." The coins clattered together again, but this time her hand trembled with fear, not temptation. "If I die, so does my son. Except he'll slowly starve to death, nursing from my lifeless body."

"Keep it," he repeated, then reached around the flames and gently closed her fingers over the coins.

She gasped. "Does that mean you won't take us?"

"It means I haven't decided yet, but either way I'm not taking your money."

Chapter Fourteen
Another Issue

"Before you give me your answer, there's something else you should know," she said as she reluctantly returned the coins to her pocket.

"What now?" he asked, his emotions so on edge he was on the verge of laughter.

"I should have done it differently. How I left." Her face took on a pained expression and she lifted her hands and then let them fall, as if all were hopeless. "William had a fresh bottle of whiskey sitting on the table at breakfast. If there was one thing I could count on with that man, it was that he'd drink all morning, be passed out by late afternoon, and wouldn't awaken until sometime the next day."

Philip clenched his jaw so tight his muscles ached at the realization she'd gotten adept at predicting and planning around her husband's worthlessness.

"I waited until the bottle slipped out of his fingers and hit the floor. I had Clark in my arms by the time it stopped rolling. On my way out the door, I snatched the letter from my aunt and the quilt off the bed. At the end of the porch steps I realized I didn't have any food, but I kept going, figuring I could forage for berries and Clark could nurse."

She paused and gave Philip an apologetic look.

"However, it turned out I was too eager. I was so focused on gathering and going that I didn't take the time to tie my own boots. Ten feet into the yard, and I heard William kicking the front door open. As I rounded the chicken coop I heard him shouting my name. I looked back. He stood at the top of the porch steps, one hand bracing himself solid against the railing and his other hand bracing the butt of the shotgun against his hip."

She trailed off, staring into the air as if reliving every moment of her flight to freedom. At first Philip thought she was overcome by shame or embarrassment. Then she sat a little straighter and smiled a little stronger, and he realized that for the first time she might be seeing the courage in her actions.

Oblivious to his observations, Hannah continued. "William yelled my name, then stumbled down the steps and fell in the dirt. Fear made me squeeze Clark too tight, and he started crying. I cried too, when I saw William rise again."

She laid her hand upon her chest, fingers splayed. "Then, God showed me I still had a chance. Three steps in, when I saw William's steps were lurching, his gait wobbly, I turned and started running. Fast. So fast one of my boots flew off. I kept going." She lowered her voice to a whisper, "I knew if I stopped, we might never leave again."

Philip considered the ambiguous comment. Either she knew she'd never have the courage to flee again, or she knew her husband would hurt her so bad she'd never be able to get away—or worse.

"Hannah," he said, holding up a halting hand. "You don't have to tell me these things."

"Actually, I do. Remember when I said there was something you needed to know before you gave me your answer?"

"Yes."

She curled her fingers around the end of the quilt. Silently, she raised the edge, exposing her bare, bloodied foot.

Chapter Fifteen
Trapper's Code

Long ago, Philip's uncle—a mountain man who'd attended many of the infamous rendezvous during the 1830s—had told him a story he'd never forgotten.

Hugh Glass, a courageous outdoorsman who'd joined a group of men on a trapping expedition, had the misfortune to come upon a mother grizzly and her cubs. She'd turned upon him and he'd had no choice but to shoot to kill. She'd proven herself to be courageous in her own right, for before she'd breathed her last breath she'd pulled Glass from the tree he'd clamored into to await her death. A brutal mauling had ensued, and moments after she'd made the last of many lacerations across his body, she'd fallen upon him, dead.

Other men had been quick to help, but it seemed his

death was eminent. They'd waited for the inevitable, but Glass had clung to life. Trappers had an unwritten code unto themselves—never leave an injured man. However the men had grown restless and eventually decided the majority would move on, leaving two men, Jim Bridger and John Fitzgerald, to stay with Glass until he died. Days later, they'd tired of waiting and abandoned him.

He'd lived.

Six weeks and two hundred grueling miles later, Glass had finally located the men from his expedition, seeking revenge on those who'd reported his body dead and buried.

Even as a child, Philip had wondered at the two men's decision to leave Glass. Wondered how'd they'd justified giving their word they'd do one thing, and then done the opposite, ensuring the solitary death of a man they'd sworn to protect until his last breath. Wondered at their thoughts during the first few steps of their betrayal. Had Glass called out to them? Pleaded for them to stay? Or had they done the worst and left while he'd slept?

Before their journey, those men had been strangers. Hannah's family—the ones who should have taken a cherishing and protecting role in her life—were the ones who'd failed her.

A concept Philip knew all too well.

A distant memory flickered to life before his eyes—his mother, weeping in the corner of the kitchen, her hand outstretched to keep her young, curious son from coming closer. Other memories intruded. Himself at twelve years old, running in from the woodshed, then standing uncertainly in the doorway as his father's shouts and his mother's fervent pleading reverberated off the walls. Finally stepping forward, his fists and courage raised. Rising from blackness with a crushing headache and finding his mother lying motionless on the floor beside the fireplace, her neck bent at an impossible angle against the stone hearth.

And that time, his father had been the one weeping in the corner.

The year before her death, his mother had pulled him into the barn, spoken in an eager whisper about her plan to escape his father's wrath. He'd spent the next year waiting for her signal, a signal she'd ultimately never given. She'd had nowhere to go.

Philip stared at Hannah's bloodied foot and thought of the years he'd spent watching his mother cowering as his father stood over her, battering her with cruel words and clenched fists. He then stared at Clark, and thought of the boy suffering the same fate he'd lived through—being raised by a father who'd killed his mother. Then he thought of how he'd spent the past eighteen years yearning for the impossible—forgiveness from a child he'd failed to protect from her own mother's wrath.

Though redemption for his past mistakes wouldn't come from helping this woman and her child, it would certainly be a start.

"Hannah, get a good night's sleep. We'll leave for Great Falls at first light."

Chapter Sixteen
Warming Up

Sunday, December 19, 1886

Philip crouched beside Hannah and nudged her awake.

"Good morning," he said when her eyes finally opened. "We leave in ten minutes, so you need to start getting ready."

If they kept a steady pace and made the fifteen miles Philip was hoping for, they'd get through the woods and end their day on the edge of the flat land. Knowing that tomorrow there'd be no trees or mountains to offer protection from the ceaseless wind, Philip asked a question he'd been wondering for some time, since he'd only seen her wrapped in a quilt.

"What clothes do you have?"

"A few things." She sat up, repositioned her awakening son, then reached down into her quilt and brought out a cotton bag no bigger than a dinner plate. She set it aside, unopened, then dug into the quilt again, this time bringing out a child's coat made of wool. Philip breathed a sigh of relief to see built-in mittens and a hood, and then another when she pulled out a pair of matching leggings that had coverings for the boy's feet.

"What about you?" he asked, almost certain her answer would mean sacrifices of his own clothes. "Do you have a coat?"

She pinched the shoulder of her sweater between her thumb and forefinger and raised it in the air. "I spun the wool and then knitted this myself last year," she said, proudly. "It's quite warm."

Philip held back a groan. Homespun yarn was no match for below-zero temperatures, or hours spent fighting a frigid wind. "What about your pants?"

She cringed. "Light cotton. Holes in both knees."

"And you only have the one boot?"

She nodded.

"Anything else in there?" he asked, nodding to her bag Clark was now pulling over his head while giggling with glee. "Hats? Gloves? Extra socks?"

She shook her head. "Only a few cloth napkins for Clark."

"I have some things to keep you warm. Let's start with these," he said, holding his moccasins in the air with his fingertips. "They'll be too big, but anything is better than nothing. Besides, at the pace I'll set you won't make it a mile with only one boot."

Her gaze went to his feet, now clad in his leather boots, and then her eyes widened as she noticed what else lay upon the ground. "It snowed?"

"Just a dusting."

"Can we still leave?" she asked, casting uneasy glances at the rocky hills now dotted with patches of white.

"Of course. The wind blows it easily, and since it's fluffy, not wet, we can shuffle right through it." Philip smiled, attempting to reassure. "My joints tell me to expect nothing more for the next few days."

Hannah nodded, then spent the next few minutes dressing Clark, who was far more interested in rolling across the dirt than he was in readying for the day. After he was clad in warmth head to toe, Hannah started to rise. Halfway up she wobbled briefly, and then dropped to her knees.

"Whoa!" Philip rushed to her side. "Let me help you."

Taking her hands—as cold as his got after he'd spent hours plunging them in frigid water, setting or retrieving his traps—he eased her to her feet. After he'd reassured himself her balance was back, he pulled his rabbit fur-lined gloves from under his belt and slid them over her fingers.

"I can't take these from you," she said, shaking her head. "What about your hands? They'll get cold."

"These meaty paws?" Philip scoffed and held up his scarred hands. "They never get cold." The lie came easily as he tugged the ends of his gloves down onto her forearms and then pulled her sweater sleeves over them. Then he shrugged free of his coat and draped it over her shoulders. To his dismay, she nearly crumpled from the weight.

"You can drape your quilt around your shoulders like a poncho," he said, reluctantly taking back his coat. "I worry about you tripping, so we'll have to watch that it doesn't drag."

Hannah nodded, then eyed the ground again. "Are you sure we can still leave today?"

"Without a doubt. Think of snow as a benefit rather than a hindrance. It allows us constant access to water." He lowered his fingers to a flat rock, scraped a few flakes together, dropped them into his mouth, and then grinned. "Anytime we're thirsty we can just grab a handful."

Hannah smiled in return, and Philip was relieved to see a glimpse of her rising trust. He declined to mention the downside of the recent snowfall. Passing through snow left easily visible tracks—good to stalk animals, but bad if a husband decided to track his wife and child.

While Hannah appeared confident he wouldn't follow, there was no guarantee he wasn't lurking somewhere close by. Watching. Waiting. However now was not the time to address that particular issue. Now was the time to put some serious miles between them and the man she'd fled.

Chapter Seventeen
Prayer

"We'll leave as soon as I make certain the fire is out." Philip kicked dirt over the fading coals, then checked the remains by stirring them with his boot heel. Satisfied, he looked to where Hannah waited with Clark in her arms. "You sure you'll be able to carry him? We got a ways to go before we're there."

"Yes, we'll be fine." Though she was nodding with confidence, she began looking around.

Philip took note of her concern for their surroundings. "Looking for something in particular?" *Or someone?*

"I was hoping you had a horse or a donkey?"

"No. Afraid not."

Her brow furrowed in disappointment. "I thought trappers used pack animals to transport their furs.

Why don't you?"

"I had a horse. A fine one. But he died last week." Philip's throat stung as he recalled how he'd woken to his horse lying in a motionless heap instead of waiting by his saddle. "I'm the sole beast of burden now."

"I'm sorry to hear that."

Philip didn't bother to clarify which made her sorry—that his horse had died, or that he was on foot.

"Me too." He cleared his throat and turned around, unwilling to show the depth of his misery.

Though other trappers and mountain men had no qualms about slaughtering their horses when their rumbling stomachs overwhelmed their need to ride, Philip had never considered taking Freddy's life. Even during the winter of 1873, when he hadn't seen bare ground for five months straight due to all the snow. Nor when he'd once spent the entire month of February huddled in a cave because the temperatures were so low he didn't dare venture far from the warmth of his meager fire.

He'd bought Freddy fresh off the riverboat to Fort Benton, from a man so hunchbacked Philip couldn't see his face, so he couldn't tell if he'd been taken advantage of or had gotten a good horse for a good deal. Turned out, it had been a little of both.

"You ready?" Philip asked, his voice gruff with melancholy.

"I need to do one more thing before we leave," Hannah replied, then bowed her head.

"Thank you, Lord, for this day you have given us and thank you for leading Philip to Clark and me in our time of need. I pray that he's capable of handling the challenges we are sure to face during the days to come, and please reward him for his willingness to put aside his own plans and take on the overwhelming task I've put upon him. In Jesus name, Amen."

Hannah opened her eyes and looked to him expectantly, but he stayed silent.

She had some nerve, praying that he was capable of doing what she'd asked. Of course he was capable! As for the nonsense of him being rewarded, she had it all wrong. He was taking her and the boy to where they needed to go, and was doing it begrudgingly at best, mostly out of guilt, but definitely not because he thought he'd earn something from a higher power.

Long ago he'd been a believer in God, but he'd quit the moment he'd seen who was in his well, and who lay beside it. And he wasn't about to start again now.

Chapter Eighteen
First Day

Philip took the lead and Hannah trudged along behind, quickly proving herself capable at walking without conversation or complaint. Though his moccasins were far too big, she managed to keep a steady pace.

Late in the afternoon, everything changed.

Hannah began stumbling. Whether it was due to uneven terrain or problems with balance, he didn't know. However, he'd seen other troubles throughout the day: blinking fast as if trying to clear her vision, answering simple questions incorrectly and with much confusion, and wincing while pressing her hand to her forehead.

As for Clark, he'd napped for several hours at a time, and didn't endlessly fret as many babies his age were known to do when forced to be carried for hours on end. His lethargy caused Philip more worry than if he'd squirmed and squalled the entire day.

The likely culprits for their troubles were hunger and exhaustion. Though he couldn't rule out complications from her obvious injuries, or Clark's suspected ones. Rest and plentiful food was the cure for their ailments, and neither was possible.

Philip had hoped to make it out of the mountains and onto the flatlands their first day, but by early evening he knew it was time to call it a day. Better to lose a few miles than deal with the troubles pushing her farther would bring.

"We've gone about thirteen miles," Philip said, shrugging free of his pack. "How about we stop?"

"Yes." With a groan of relief, she tipped back her head and rolled the quilt off her shoulders. It landed in the dirt with a heavy thud. "Let me know what I can do to help set up camp," she said, adjusting Clark in her arms. "I'd offer to cook, but…"

"I don't have any food worth cooking," he said, finishing her criticism. "It's because before I met you I was traveling light and moving fast, so I had no time to hunt for meat or fish." Bristling at her ingratitude, he flung open his pack and dug around for what little pemmican and jerky he had left.

"No, it isn't that at all," she murmured, putting up her hand in protest. "I was going to say that William always said I was a bad cook, so I'm not too confident in my ability."

Philip stared at her hand, now shaking like a leaf in a hurricane, then bowed his head to hide his shame. He'd jumped to a conclusion before hearing all the facts, and even worse, he'd scared her again. The fact that he'd lived like a hermit for so long that he wasn't used to interacting with people anymore was no excuse.

Hannah continued on, oblivious to his regrets. "William was always so adamant that his meals be on the table at certain times, and I did my best, even though he was usually so late it would be cold by the time he sat down. Inevitably he'd end up throwing his plate up against the wall, saying what I considered edible was flavorless slop, unfit for even our dog."

Remorse overwhelmed him and he couldn't allow one more second to pass without speaking up.

"Hannah, I'm sorry for what I just said, and how I acted." Clasping his hands together, he pointed both index fingers to her. "You were about to make a wonderful offer, and I had no call to snap at you how I did."

"It's all right," she said. "I know you didn't mean it. Besides, it's been a long day and you're tired."

"No. It's not all right." His stomach soured at how quick she was to make excuses for him. Probably an old habit by now, born of years of placating an irrational, raging husband. "I was wrong and I'm sorry. I will do my best to never let it happen again."

As a tentative smile flitted across her lips in a show of acceptance of his apology and promise, Philip wondered how many times she'd heard the same words from her husband.

"How long were you with him?" he asked.

"Two years." She paused, then shrugged. "I think it's like the fable of the frog in the water. If you drop a frog in boiling water it'll jump right out. But if you put it in cold water and gradually heat it to boiling, it stays."

She ran a fingertip along Clark's cheek, and then looked to Philip.

"No matter how hard I tried, I couldn't make him happy. According to him, I never did anything right when it came to running a household. Laundry, cleaning, cooking. He wanted things done a certain way, on a certain day, and viewed anything less as disobedience worthy of a slap. At a minimum."

Philip forced his expression to remain neutral, but on the inside he seethed to throttle the man who'd instilled such insecurities in Hannah. She'd become so eager to please she'd lost sight of herself. Instead of giving her empty reassurances of her capabilities, he did the one thing he was certain her husband had never done—put her needs first.

"The only thing you need to focus on tonight is taking care of your boy. I'll handle everything else."

"Thank you," she murmured, sinking to the ground.

"I know it's too heavy for you to wear while walking," he said, slipping free of his coat and then settling it around her shoulders, "but I'd like you to have it at night."

"Are you sure?" she asked.

"I insist. I've spent so many years out in the wild, the cold barely affects me anymore." Untrue, but his future suffering was worth the sight of her snuggling Clark within the instant warmth Philip's lingering body heat provided. Without another word, he unwound his bundle of furs. Working quickly, he laid two made beavers on the ground to act as a protective barrier against cold and moisture, then he spread out the sole antelope pelt. He fetched her quilt, shook out the dirt, then laid it over the furs. It was a crude, yet cozy bedroll.

"Now I'll make a smaller one for Clark," he said, heading toward his furs.

"Thank you, but I prefer to hold him close."

Philip nodded his understanding, and then headed out to gather wood.

****

An hour later a stack of branches sat near the fire ring, and flames danced before them in the impending twilight.

By heating water and simmering half of the remaining pemmican, Philip made a broth that satisfied no one, but was better than nothing. He had to force himself to drink his share; two lives depended upon him and he needed to keep his strength. If he failed, they all failed.

After the dishes were collected, wiped clean, and stored away in his pack, Hannah sat beneath the cover of the quilt, trying yet again to convince an uncooperative Clark to nurse.

"How's he doing?" Philip asked.

Though at the beginning of the day they'd both been uncomfortable discussing something that was considered private between a mother and child, by that afternoon they'd both abandoned restraint in their discussions about Clark. When fighting for a life, practicality took priority over propriety.

"He's got to be hungry—he hasn't nursed in hours—but he keeps pushing me away." Hannah rested her forehead against her palm and closed her eyes against the tears slipping down her cheeks. "I don't know what else to do."

Knowing firsthand how a baby could sense their mother's stress, Philip made a suggestion. "Why don't you take a break? Try again later?"

Hannah gave a weary nod, then after a few practiced

adjustments, she lowered the quilt. Clark sat upon her lap, his eyes wide to the world around him. During the switch of positions, his green scrap of cloth fluttered to the ground. It lay, unnoticed by Hannah, within inches of Clark's grasp. He hesitated, then reached out his right arm to retrieve it. Whimpers began within seconds, but Philip wasn't certain they stemmed from the loss of his special blanket, or something else.

"What's wrong?" Hannah crooned, looking over her boy and then her surroundings. Her eyes brightened upon catching sight of cloth. "He's had this since the day he was born," she said, then picked it up and placed it in her son's lap. "He gets fussy when it's not close."

On a hunch, Philip held a precious piece of jerky in front of the boy's right side, then watched carefully as the boy shifted his weight to reach with his left hand. Philip grimaced as his suspicions were confirmed.

"I know you don't have a lot of that left," she said. "I'll try and feed him again."

He dared an unbidden observation. "It's hard for a baby to concentrate on taking nourishment if they're in pain."

Her stare turned cold. "I'm doing the best I can."

"I know." Philip hesitated, then forged ahead, figuring he might as well be out with it all. "Of course, there's always another consideration."

"What's that?" she asked, warily.

"It's hard for a mother to provide nourishment if she's in pain."

"You're very astute," she said, her eyes showing her resignation to the truth in his words. "How is it you know of such things?"

Philip chose to purposely misinterpret the last sentence. "I've had experience tending to injuries, both my own and those of men I've come across over the years."

Hannah's nod stemmed more from politeness than interest, so he chose his words wisely. "I'd like to help you and your boy."

Hannah shook her head. "We're fine, thank you."

He disagreed, but chose not to push. For now.

Chapter Nineteen
Notions and Recollections

Monday, December 20, 1886

"Watch your step," Philip said, pointing to a moss-covered rock where Hannah was about to step. "Might be slippery."

She sidestepped the rock, then paused to unwind Clark's fingers from her hair for the fifth time that morning.

"Braiding your hair might keep his fingers out of it," he suggested after they'd started walking again. "I have a brush you could borrow."

"Thank you. I'll do it tonight." Hannah studied him for a moment, then smiled. "You're nothing like I thought a trapper would be."

"What did you expect?" he asked, curious how he'd

changed her preconceived notions.

"Long hair. Bad teeth. Mean. No schooling. Shun society."

He'd been eager to distract Hannah from her worries and rumbling stomach. And if there was one certain way to distract a woman, it was talking. "The shunning society part is fairly accurate, but the rest?" He chuckled. "Not so much."

"How is it your teeth aren't worn down to brown stubs? Or gone?"

He reached into his possibles bag, brought out his bone-handled toothbrush, and ran his thumb along the worn-down bristles. "I go through one of these every year."

"How come your hair isn't a knotted, filthy mess that ends at the middle of your back?"

"Soap and a brush do wonders if you make the effort. As for the length?" He lifted a hunk of his hair with one hand, while his other hand pretended to run a knife just above the ends. "I hack it off when it starts hanging in my food while I'm cooking, or eating."

"What about your beard?"

"Keeps my face warm. Neck too." He patted the possibles bag. "I got a straight razor and a mirror in here. Figure if I ever get a hankering to impress a woman, giving myself a smooth shave will be the first thing I do."

"Schooling?"

"Education gave me knowledge. Solitary life gave me wisdom."

She pondered that for a moment, then asked the one question he'd figured would come sooner or later. "What about drinking?"

"Never took to the idea." Years ago, his uncle had spoken of attending annual rendezvous where trappers willingly lost a year's worth of wages during a week's worth of debauchery. Rendezvous were long gone now, but he'd seen the same behaviors from trappers at trading posts. Philip wanted no part of such nonsense.

He stopped at the crest of their last rugged peak and looked down upon the grasslands that marked the beginning of the next part of their journey. While the gentle rise and fall of the hills ahead would be easier to navigate, they'd be battling strong winds until they reached the front door of their destination.

Both he and Hannah repositioned their burdens, and then Philip led them off again. He'd enjoyed their camaraderie, so he asked a question guaranteed to get Hannah talking again.

"How did Clark get his name?"

Her eyes gleamed with pride. "I chose it. He's named after the explorer, William Clark, in the hopes that he'll grow up and do great things for the nation and never settle for mediocrity." Her expression turned grave. "I also hope he'll eventually forgive his mother for not having the sense to see the truth of his father's character before it was too late."

"What did your husband think of your choice?"

"He didn't care about a name. All he cared about was that I'd birthed a boy." She scoffed. "Less than ten minutes after Clark arrived, William told me he was sick of cooking his own meals and listening to all the moaning and carrying on I'd been doing for the past day and a half. He ordered me to get cleaned up and to have dinner on the table within the hour."

Philip's stomach roiled with disgust that a man could be so callous. When he'd stared down at his own wife, holding his daughter in her arms after an exhausting fight to bring her into the world, all he could think about was how much he wanted to love and protect them both.

"Was it ever good between you two?" he asked.

"In the beginning he was nice. Tender. Affectionate. Brought me flowers. Smiled a lot. Convinced me to do things I knew I shouldn't. Then, one night in an empty barn stall, he wouldn't listen, and..."

Philip said nothing, because there was nothing he could say to take away the pain that came from a betrayal so despicable. The only thing he could do for her was to keep listening.

She gave him a weak smile and then motioned to Clark, who again had his left hand clutched around a lock of her hair. "That was also the night God began the greatest treasure in my life."

As they walked shoulder to shoulder for another hundred yards, Philip wavered between staying silent and an overwhelming sense that she'd had no one to talk to for so long she was eager to tell her story, even to a near stranger. He took the risk.

"What about your parents? Did you tell them what happened?"

"Father caught us minutes after it was over. He was livid. Dragged us both into the house. I tried to say how I was forced, but he wouldn't listen. He slapped me across the cheek, said I was soiled. He demanded I marry William immediately."

"What about your mother?"

Hannah snorted. "She was weak. Always deferred to him on everything. Never stood up for what she wanted. She kept agreeing with my father, even when he said since I'd succumbed to temptation it was my duty to be with William. Forever. When my father forced William back out to the barn to help him hitch up the wagon, I sank to my knees in front of her. I told her everything and then pleaded with her not to make me go."

"What did she do?"

Blinking fast and swallowing hard, she made it another ten feet before she'd collected herself enough to answer. "Packed my bags, dropped them on the front porch, pushed me outside, and then slammed the door. I was numb from all that had happened, all that I'd lost. I was only fifteen, with nowhere else to go. My father drove us into town, woke up the preacher, and William and I were married within the hour."

Hannah's pace quickened, as if she took strength from putting one foot in front of the other, each step bringing her farther away from her husband and closer to a new life. After a hundred more yards her spine was straighter and her jaw was set.

"Two years later, and here I am. Some might think I've got no one left to count on, but that's not true. I have my aunt again, and of course I have something that will never let me down."

"What?"

"My faith." Hannah's voice was quiet, but her tone was fierce, adamant. "I've been disappointed by so many people in my life, but I'm still willing to believe the good in people. I'm still willing to trust that you're here to help me. Help us," she corrected, looking down at her son. "And most of all, I am willing to trust in God that he'll see me through this difficult time." She gazed to the sky, and then to him. "After all, he already sent you."

Philip scoffed at such an outlandish notion. "Hogwash."

Hannah didn't challenge him, or admonish him for the insult he already regretted. Instead, she simply stared at him, her expression suddenly curious. "What about you? What brought you to live out here?"

Chapter Twenty
Why

"What brought me to live out here?" he repeated her question as he debated how much sorrow he wanted to share. "A steamboat."

Her raised eyebrow told of her expectation for expansion.

"I'd grown up listening to my uncle's stories of fur trappers and their wild adventures out west, so in 1868 I hopped aboard a steamboat headed for Fort Benton." Aside from the crew's constant rehashing of one particular tale—how the year prior the governor, Union General Thomas Francis Meagher, had fallen overboard from a steamboat and drowned—the journey had been uneventful.

"If I'd have had a lick of sense I would have cared more that there were already too many trappers and not enough beavers. Or that prices for beaver pelts had fallen for the past twenty years since silk was on the rise as a replacement."

He ran his palm along his forehead, smoothing back sweaty curls. "So, though I knew nothing about trapping except that the entire industry was on the verge of collapse, I decided to give it a try. I was stubborn enough to keep trying until I learned what I needed to know."

In truth, he'd had a disastrous first year in the wild. He'd almost died twice, but eventually he'd learned where to buy what he needed, how to make what he couldn't trade for, and over the next few years he developed strong relationships with the trading posts in the area and became profitable enough to keep going.

"Did you find what you were seeking?"

He assumed she meant money. "Enough to get me a cabin where I can sit comfortable on my porch and await the inevitable. I'm too old for anything else."

"Hogwash," she said.

After they shared a chuckle at her use of his previous insult, though hers was in jest, she sobered. "I should clarify my earlier question. You left everything to live in a desolate place. Why?"

Philip grimaced. On his wedding day, he'd held the hand of a woman he'd known for two weeks and pledged to love her for the rest of his life. She'd made the same pledge, but over the next few months she'd grown bitter and spiteful toward him. A year later, she'd acted the same toward their daughter. Two years later, he'd returned from a hunting trip and found a note on the kitchen table, his daughter's body down the well, and his wife's beside it. One week later he'd left for Fort Benton.

"I figured it was the best place to disappear to while I tried to forget something," he finally answered.

"Has it worked?"

"Unfortunately, no."

Chapter Twenty-One
Another Offer of Help

Philip helped Hannah to her feet for the third time that afternoon. She accepted, again making a litany of excuses for what had caused her to stumble—the grass was too long, the fluttering of the quilt in the wind had startled her, or Clark had shifted in her arms and threw off her stride.

Philip knew different.

He placed a steadying hand upon her shoulder and made another surreptitious evaluation of the wound on her left temple—the likely reason behind her troubles. There was also her foot to consider. Infection may have set in and moved well up her leg by now. And given the way he'd seen her wince when Clark had dug his feet into her ribs he wouldn't be surprised if her husband had taken a go at her torso when he'd given her the last beating.

Tonight he needed to be firm with her about tending to her injuries.

"Do you want me to hold Clark for a while?" He kept his tone light, but he dreaded adding another twenty pounds to his arms.

"No," she replied, her ashen face fierce with resolve. "I can take care of him."

While his throbbing back was relieved at her rugged determination, his mind worried over what would happen if one day she collapsed and couldn't rise again. Since there was no other option but to go on, Philip started walking. However, he took great care to position himself within reach of Hannah's arm and waist in case she faltered again. A precaution that proved worthy less than half an hour later.

Philip caught her by the waist just as she went forward, turning what should have been a nose-busting dive into merely a clumsy lowering to her knees. He pulled her to her feet again and then let her go, but kept his hands close. To his dismay, Clark remained quiet.

"Thank you," she murmured, putting her hand to her forehead and closing her eyes. Seconds later, she swayed and fell against him.

"How about we call it a day?" he asked, unwilling to risk her taking even one more step.

She stared up at him, panic in her eyes. "If we do, won't that put us at risk of not making my aunt's house by Christmas?"

They'd gone about fourteen miles that day, and he wasn't concerned about meeting Hannah's self-imposed deadline. His main concern—aside from convincing her to let him examine her injuries—was running out of food. A grown man could survive for long stretches on only water, but a nursing mother and a baby were a different story. Right now there was enough jerky for each to have a thumb-sized hunk for three more breakfasts and enough pemmican for two more dinners of the watery broth he'd made the night before. He had no idea what they'd eat during the last days of the journey.

One thing was in their favor; his canteens were both full.

"We covered a lot of ground today, so how about we call it a day?" he repeated, lowering her to the ground even as she still considered her answer.

Hannah bit her lip and fought back tears. "I'd like that very much."

"We'll make camp right here," he said, his easy demeanor hiding his inner worry over the amount of miles they had left to reach Great Falls—at least forty-five—and how many miles they could have covered from now until twilight—at least three—when he'd originally planned on stopping. However, looking at Hannah and the relief apparent on her pale face, he concluded he'd made the right choice.

He let out a long groan as he dropped his furs and pack to the ground. After a few arm-to-the-sky stretches to work the kinks from his back, he dug into his possibles bag and brought out a brush and a small length of thin leather. He set them on the ground beside her, then eyed her tangled hair. "I got quite proficient at braiding my horse's tail over the years. Let me know if you need any help."

While he worked to replicate the bedroll he'd made for her and Clark the previous night, he considered how she'd handled the day. She'd never complained, never questioned his ability or his decisions, she'd simply put one foot in front of the other and followed his lead. Her rising compliance during the late afternoon worried him more than answering any question she'd asked him that morning. Hunger and exhaustion were already sapping her strength, and they still had many hard days ahead.

Once she was settled beneath his coat and had Clark resting comfortably on her lap, he trudged off. After gathering an armload of small branches off a cluster of shrubs he'd had to walk nearly a quarter-mile to find, he returned. He pulled two pinecones from the dwindling stash in his coat pocket, and then brought out his flint. Within a minute he was blowing on the beginnings of a fire, and within five the flames were strong enough to warm chilled hands. He poured water into the pot and set it near the ring.

"Once the fire dies down I'll put this on to boil. Broth will be ready in about half an hour, but in the meantime here's some water." He filled a tin cup and passed it over. She took several sips, then shared with Clark.

"He's doing so great," she said, smiling as he took another drink. "He's been so cooperative all day; barely fussy at all anymore."

Philip nodded, but in truth he viewed the boy's sluggish temperament as a problem, not a benefit. Clark, like his mother, was showing signs of exhaustion. And pain.

"How's his arm?" Philip asked, rolling the tip of his beard between his thumb and forefinger.

His question caught her with the water cup halfway to her mouth. With a deliberateness that showed her fear of waste, she slowly set the cup on the ground by her knee. Once it was out of her way, she focused on Philip. "You've noticed?"

"Hard not to," he replied. "I know you're having troubles too."

Her fingers grazed the lines across her throat, then she kissed the top of Clark's head. "You're already doing so much, sacrificing so much. I didn't want to bother you any further."

"Watching you and your boy suffer is heartbreaking, even more so because I have the skills to heal, or at least relieve some of the pain. Let me help you," he added quietly, sensing her trust in him was at a vital turning point.

At long last, Hannah nodded.

Chapter Twenty-Two
Confession

Philip dug through his possibles bag and brought out everything he anticipated he'd need to help them. His supply bag was next. Clark sat on his mother's lap, his head leaning against her chest, and both of them watched Philip with wide-eyed interest as the collection grew to include herbs, a handkerchief, long thin lengths of cloth strips, a sewing needle, and two types of salves.

"Did you train to be a doctor before you became a trapper?"

"No," he replied, dampening a cloth square with a few drops of water. "I learned out of necessity. If a man wants to stay alive out here for any length of time, he needs to know a few things about doctoring because it's inevitable to come across broken bones, deep cuts that need cleaning out and then stitching, and an end-less variety of internal ailments."

He eyed the gash on her cheek, frowned, and then set aside the needle.

"There's no medicine or chloroform for hundreds, if not thousands, of miles. Out here herbal remedies are reliable, and easy to come by if you know where to look." Philip gave her a confident look, hoping to re-assure her that he wouldn't do more harm than good. "I'm ready to begin."

She didn't move.

"You've got nothing to be embarrassed about, and no need to hide anything from me."

As she reluctantly began to shrug free of his coat, she jostled Clark's right arm. Within seconds, both were crying.

"Let's do this a different way." Eager to put her at ease again, he made an exaggerated show of relaxing against his bundle of furs, lacing his hands together behind his head, and crossing his feet at the ankle. "How about instead we start with you telling me as much as you can recall about how you and Clark got your injuries?"

Her sigh of relief and returning sense of calm was short-lived. "Why do you need to know details?" Her expression turned defiant, scornful. "Isn't it enough that I survived everything he doled out? That I saved my boy?"

Her anger made sense. To her, at this moment, he was just another person in her life demanding something she didn't want to give without a care for her feelings. Instead of being hurt by her tone, he rejoiced. He wanted her to nurture that newfound willingness to challenge orders, wanted her to burn with indignation at what her own husband had done to her and her son. If she never forgot what he'd done, she'd never go back to him. Even if he promised to change.

Philip knew firsthand, since he'd suffered for years from a father who would rage for an hour, then spend the next hour making tearful excuses and solemn vows to never hurt him or his mother again. His mother always had always taken him back, always believed his lies of wanting to be a better husband to her and a better father to his son.

Until the next beating.

"Hannah, no matter what your husband has said or done to convince you otherwise, he had no call to put his hands on you in anger."

She tilted her head to the side, studying him for so long he finally succumbed to the urge to confess at least one of his secrets to someone who understood.

"Hannah, there's a reason I know so much about what you've gone through. Why I keep saying how brave you are for leaving." His voice broke, but he forced himself to continue in a whisper. "I endured the life you've saved Clark from living."

Chapter Twenty-Three
Reliving

They never spoke of his confession again, but from that moment a strong bond of familiarity was forged. When he collected his emotions, Philip abandoned the exam to make their broth, and during the meager dinner their talk centered on weather, the terrain they'd encounter in the coming days, and even a few stories from his first years of trapping. After they'd shared laughter at his mistakes, Philip scrubbed the pot clean. When everything was put away, he looked to Hannah and motioned to the waiting medical supplies.

"How much do you need to know?" she asked, resigned to the fact that she needed his help.

"Tell me enough so I can figure out where to look, and what to look for when I do. How about we start with Clark?" Philip made an elaborate gesture of tapping his own right arm, first at the elbow then the shoulder. "How'd his arm get hurt?"

A tear slid down her cheek and she scrubbed it away, as if angry to have cried even one more time because of her husband.

"William spent little time with his son, yet considered himself the sole and final authority on raising him. He refused to help with Clark's day-to-day care, but when he viewed Clark as doing anything he deemed unacceptable—crying for what he considered to be too long, making a mess with his toys, basically everything a normal child would do—he'd intervene with punishments. Things like slapping his hands or his cheek, or holding him in the air and shouting corrections inches from his face. He viewed what he did as right, because that's the way he was raised." Hannah stared at the flames, almost as if in a trance. "I would just sit there—motionless and mute—and watch."

"There was nothing you could have done," Philip said.

"You're wrong." Her voice was simplistic, childlike. "What I did was even worse than doing nothing. I rationalized."

"I don't understand."

"Me neither." She snapped from her daze and fixed a challenging stare at Philip. "I don't understand how I'd watch William scream at our son until both were shaking, one with rage and one with fear, and I'd rationalize how at least there was one thing I could take comfort in—that William never hit him. Eventually, I had to rationalize how when he hit, it wasn't too hard."

Though Hannah was telling him way more than she needed to, and nothing so far would give him insight into their current injuries, Philip decided not to stop her. Unburdening herself of the stories she carried was helpful in a different way.

"Then, last week Clark was crying because he was getting a new tooth. William was drinking, as usual. Suddenly, he said that a boy needed to learn young how to be tough. He grabbed him out of my arms—I let go because I was worried hanging onto him would hurt him worse—opened the front door, and tossed him onto the porch."

Philip held back a grimace. Even his own father hadn't been so ruthless.

"It was long past sunset, and so cold. Clark wasn't dressed for the weather—he wore only a light nightshirt made of thin cotton. Even worse, he'd gotten adept at crawling and every way off the porch was dangerous. The railings were wide enough for him to slip through and the steps were only five feet away from the door."

Eyes on Philip, she steepled her fingers together, then tapped them against her lips several times before continuing.

"I knew I had to get to him, fast, but every time I tried to get past William he punched me—face, stomach, head—anywhere and everywhere. With each hit he told me everything was my fault. That I'd raised our son to be a whiner who cried at everything, and that he needed to be toughened up if he was going to grow up to be a man worth respecting. And since I wasn't raising him right, he would."

She dropped her face in her hands. "Clark's cries turned to panicked screams, but I never got past William. My son was out there, scared and alone, and I didn't help him!"

Philip couldn't stay silent a moment longer. "You *couldn't* help him, because someone wouldn't let you. There's a big difference."

Hannah shrugged off his correction. "Eventually William got sick of hitting me, and flung the door open himself. He stomped right past Clark, who'd cried so hard he'd gotten sick all over himself. Thankfully the dog had come up from under the porch. Bruno curled himself around Clark, providing the warmth and protection I couldn't give."

She smoothed her hair from her forehead and tucked it behind her ears. "For the first time, as I sat on the hearth and warmed Clark's chilled fingers and toes, I saw it all so clearly. I'd spent the past six months rationalizing how hard my husband hit our child. Hit me. I'd become the frog in the boiling water. Right then I started planning my escape. Started gathering things in a burlap bag that I knew I'd need to make the journey to my aunt's: food, warm clothes, a knife, my boots and heaviest coat." She let out a bitter laugh. "I hid the bag far under the bed, for fear he'd discover it one day and question me." Another bitter laugh. "William noticed nothing. I might as well have kept it next to the front door he was so wrapped up in himself and his sinful pursuits of liquor and willing flesh."

"What made you finally decide to leave?" Philip asked.

"I thought I had more time. I figured I'd take the winter and put away what I could, and come spring I'd set out for my aunt's house. Then, Friday morning, this happened." She gestured to her broken lip, then her temple, still crusted over with dried blood.

A dull ache began low in Philip's gut. He dreaded what he was about to hear, but he was the one who'd asked to know how they'd gotten their injuries. The best thing he could do while she told her story was to keep doing what he'd been doing—sit still, shut his mouth, and listen.

"I'd woken early and done the week's baking. Biscuits, two pies, and several loaves of bread. When I was almost finished, William got out of bed. He was mad because I didn't have coffee ready, but I was so busy with the baking and trying to keep Clark quiet I'd plumb forgotten."

"Understandable, given all you were doing for your family," Philip said.

"William didn't think that way. He got upset when I asked him to keep Clark—who was crawling around and getting into everything—busy for a minute or two, long enough for me to pull the last loaf from the oven, put away the dry ingredients, and scrape clean all the bowls and pans I'd used. To this day I don't know why I asked him to watch out for Clark." She paused, reconsidered her recollection. "I think I thought if he felt responsible, included, he'd eventually strive to be a better father."

Philip shook his head, disgusted. William had what many men wanted more than anything—a family to love, and be loved by. He had a house, a child, and a wife to grow old with, yet he'd allowed drink and temper to ruin it all.

Hannah continued. "The bread was steaming hot and William had to know that since he watched me pull it from the oven. But he tore off a chunk and gave it to Clark anyway. Clark was hungry, so he had it stuffed halfway into his mouth before I was able to cross the room and pull it free. By then, he'd burned his lips and mouth—not bad enough to disfigure, but painful all the same."

Her voice cracked and she put her hand to her throat. Wordlessly, he offered his canteen. "Thank you," she murmured, handing it back to him.

"What happened next?" he asked.

"The screaming and shouting began. Clark screamed in pain, William shouted at me for being a bad mother who didn't watch our child enough, and for letting him run wild. Then, when Clark wouldn't stop crying, William slapped him across the face. Of course, that made him cry harder, which made William madder, so he grabbed Clark's right arm and raised him into the air, shaking him as he lifted. The louder Clark screamed the harder William shook. Until I found my voice, found my courage, and I shouted that he'd had enough."

She wiped her cheeks dry with the back of her hand.

"William dropped Clark to the floor and I sank to my knees beside him. I immediately knew something was wrong with his arm. Something that couldn't be fixed with cuddles and time. He needed a doctor."

"Let me guess. Your husband disagreed."

"I'd never seen him so angry. Though I'd never been so angry with him either. He was shouting how he wouldn't allow his wife to challenge his authority or his decisions for his family. I was shouting for him to find a doctor. I begged him, saying I was sure he hadn't meant to hurt Clark. A lie, of course, but by then I was ready to say anything, do anything, because what mattered most was getting Clark help. William still refused, saying he wasn't going to have no backwoods doctor judging how he ran his household."

She kept back tears by taking three deep, cleansing breaths, then continued. "I finally told him what he was really afraid of was having another man judge him for hurting his own son. That's when he came after me. Fists all over me. Hard. Then he choked me for so long everything went dark. I don't know how long I was unconscious, but when I woke Clark was asleep on the floor beside me, and William was gone."

"And that's when you'd had enough," Philip said.

Hannah nodded, her eyes gleaming with pride. "That's when I'd had enough. I laid there with my son curled next to me, hoping he wasn't going to be left disfigured due to untended injuries. I envisioned my future. My son's future. William wouldn't forget what I'd done—finally stood up to him. I knew he'd spend the rest of his life trying to beat the strength I'd found that day right back out of me. I knew that eventually, I might not survive a beating. I knew my death meant William would be responsible for raising Clark on his own. I wouldn't be there to protect him."

She trailed off, overcome with emotion. He offered the canteen again, which she took. After a few sips she passed it back, then stared at him with a look that touched his very soul.

"I knew that if I didn't leave, my baby might one day grow up to be like his father." Her words were whispered, but firm. "I couldn't wait for spring. I had to leave that day."

"Good for you." Philip felt like standing and cheering for this young woman who'd overcome so much, but settled for grinning at her instead.

"I was bad off. I was so dizzy it took me three tries just to sit up. Standing was worse. I couldn't see out of my left eye. My lip was so split I couldn't talk. I had to walk with my fingers trailing over furniture and the walls to keep my balance, but I managed to wrap a towel around my head to stop the bleeding. Then I cooked a huge lunch. I set the table, and placed the fresh bottle he'd gotten from the neighbor's still that morning beside his plate. I wanted his belly full and his bottle empty by late afternoon."

A smart, solid plan.

"Sure enough, he came back right around lunchtime like nothing was wrong. Like my shirt wasn't covered with so much dried blood that my sleeve had turned brown. No, he didn't say a word, just sat and stuffed his mouth full of all I'd made. I was so nervous and my lip and head hurt so bad I could only take a few bites. Same for Clark. Then, like I told you earlier, the moment his head hung low onto his chest and that bottle hit the floor, I fled. If I could do it all over again, I would have been better prepared. I would have remembered the bag I'd stuffed under the bed. I would have waited until I was fully recovered from his beating. I would have stopped at the edge of the porch and freed Bruno from his chain so he could follow us."

While Philip had initially berated her decision to the leave when she had, after hearing her story he now knew she'd done the right thing. For herself and for her child.

"Some would say if I could do it over again, I might as well never have met William." Her expression turned wistful and she bent to kiss her son's cheek. "But then I wouldn't have Clark." She let out a long, weary sigh. "Do you know enough now?"

"Yes." He marveled at their differences. During his struggles, he'd turned away from God, whereas Hannah had kept her faith through everything. She was a true believer and he admired her resolve. Though he wondered if she'd ever wavered. After a brief hesitation, he gave in to his curiosity. "Did you ever question how God could have allowed for William to hurt you and Clark?"

"Sometimes," she replied. "Then I'd think of my favorite verse, Romans 8:31. 'If God be for us, who can be against us'?" Her lips settled into a gentle smile.

"When I finally found the gumption to leave, God brought me something I needed the most."

"What?" he asked.

"You," she replied, her teasing tone showing she thought it was the most obvious thing in the world.

Just that morning he'd given the idea an outright rebuff. Thought it outlandish and called it hogwash. However, seeing how confident Hannah was with her faith, especially given her past, perhaps there was a point to reconsidering the idea of trusting in God.

Chapter Twenty-Four
Discovering the Extent

"Well," he stammered, uncertain where to begin after her lengthy confession. To his relief, Hannah took the lead.

"I think you'll check me over first. Clark can watch you work and he'll see there's nothing to be afraid of when it's his turn."

Her tone was kind, but the look in her eyes reminded him of a mother grizzly willing to do anything to protect her young. He wasn't fooled by her reasoning for the exam order either. He understood the unspoken contract that she'd go first to see if he was competent enough to trust with her son. An odd thing to consider at this point since both her and Clark's lives were in his hands.

After she'd set Clark beside her leg and Philip had

given him a spoon to entertain himself with, it was time to begin.

"Let's work from the top down. My biggest concern is the hit you took to the head." He hadn't seen her bring back up a meal or blink away blurred images since first meeting her, but it was worth confirming. "I know you've had troubles with your stomach and your vision, but my guess is both have returned to normal by now?"

She nodded.

"Good," he replied, eager to reassure her of good news, especially when the bad was about to begin. "Your balance is still an issue, and I need you to tell me immediately if you feel faint or your headaches cause vision trouble."

Next, he flushed out the gash on her cheek and the split in her lip, then smeared a heavy layer of salve on both. When he was done, he held his fingers in the air near her throat.

"May I?" he asked.

"Yes."

Gently, he ran his fingers over her windpipe and around her neck, then gave a sigh of relief to find the surrounding muscles only swollen. "I'm thinking your voice will remain raspy for a few more weeks, but it should eventually return to normal."

Now onto the more difficult area, where he knew for

a fact trouble loomed.

"Based on how I've seen you gasp and pull away when Clark scrambles around on your right side, I think there's a problem with one of your ribs." Her mouth dropped open, and he held up his hand to stave off her worries. "Given how active you've been, I guarantee it's not broken. But I'd like to check to make sure. Did he hit your stomach? Your side?"

"Yes." Eyes downcast, she shrugged free of his coat.

Sensitive to her anxiety of allowing a strange man to touch her, he began a tender, yet thorough, exam of her torso. When he finished, he took his last cotton shirt from his pack and began ripping it into long, wide strips.

"What are you doing that for? All my cuts have long since dried up."

"Two of your ribs are bruised, and I'm worried one on your right side is cracked. I'll bind them tight; it will help with the pain." And help protect her if she fell again. If she broke a rib, a bone splinter could pierce her lung. Hating himself for what he had to ask her to do next, he raised the first cloth. "This will work better if it's against your skin."

Silently she lifted her sweater and then the shirt beneath, stopping just below her chest. Working carefully but quickly, Philip began binding her ribs. The hardest part of the task was blinking back the sudden rush of tears when he sighted the plethora of bruises on her stomach, side, and back. The man who'd done this to her deserved a beating from someone his own size. As he listened to Hannah attempt to cover her gasps and groans while he worked, Philip knew he would happily take the job.

When he finished with her ribs, he helped lower her shirt and sweater over the bandage. After a brief inspection and thorough cleaning of her foot, he was able to simply salve it, wrap it, and move on.

"Almost done." He stared at the waiting sewing needle, then looked to Hannah. "I can't stitch up the cut on your cheek, or your lip. They've been open for too long, and there's too great a risk for infection. The salve will help them heal, and hopefully the scars will be small."

Hannah dismissed his words with an impatient wave her hand. "My son's health and wellbeing is a far greater concern to me than something as superficial as scars." She glanced at Clark, who was busy tapping the spoon on the ground and chortling at the muddy mess he'd created. "You really think you can fix his arm?

"I'll try my best. I hope I'm wrong, but I think he might have a dislocated shoulder."

"What if you're right?"

"I coax it into place," Philip said, thinking how that sounded so much easier than the reality of what he'd have to do. "No use worrying until we know what we've got to worry about. Let me feel around a bit and then we'll know more."

Hannah placed Clark on her lap, and Philip sat cross-legged on the ground before them.

"Hi, little guy," he said, forcing false cheer into his tone. "How about we play a matching game?"

Clark's stare was wide, unblinking.

Keeping his motions slow and his voice high, Philip set about gaining the boy's trust by making a game of feeling around the bones and muscles of his good arm, the left. Giggles and smiles were plentiful during the process, and by the end the boy was pulling on Philip's beard and bouncing in his mother's lap.

Checking over the right arm required firm prods by Philip's swift fingers, a handkerchief for Hannah and Clark's tears, and a hefty dose of patience for them all. Then, once Clark's sobs had subsided and he and Hannah could easily hear each other again, he gave her the best news of the day.

"It's not as bad as I thought," Philip said, rejoicing in avoiding the horror of twisting a child's shoulder back into its socket, or setting a broken collarbone. "His shoulder muscles were stretched too far. However, I don't think the damage is permanent. I'm going to position his arm against his chest, then bandage it so it's immobile. After we arrive, I'll check it again and before I go I'll show you a few stretches that will help regain his strength."

Together they worked on his arm, and when it was done they exchanged weary, yet happy smiles to see the boy not fussing at the restraint.

"You did great," she said, snuggling Clark to her chest and giving him endless kisses on his forehead and cheeks. She then looked to Philip. "As did you."

****

Later that night, as Clark nursed for the first time all day, Philip made a smaller bedroll right next to Hannah's. "I know you like to hold him, but this will be better for his arm since you won't be jostling him, inadvertently of course, while you sleep."

Clark finished nursing and immediately fell asleep. Philip helped transfer him from Hannah's lap into his new bed, then covered him with enough furs to keep him warm throughout the night.

"I admit, I'm looking forward to sleeping with my arms free." She picked up the brush Philip had set out earlier and began working on a lock of hair. "It's surprising how much he wiggles during the night."

Once her hair was brushed, braided, and the end secured with the leather tie, she gave Philip the universal look all women got when they were about to pry into topics that were none of their business, while seeking out details men would rather have left alone.

Chapter Twenty-Five
Prying

"You're good with children," she said, tilting her head to the side as if trying to see him in a different light. "Do you have any of your own?"

Philip hesitated, not wanting to lie, but also not wanting to elaborate. "Not anymore."

Her brow furrowed at his purposely muddled reply, but she didn't press him further. His relief was short-lived, however, when he heard her next question.

"Do you have a wife?"

"Not anymore," he repeated, hoping the same reply to her different question, combined with his reluctant tone, would convince her to quit prying. It almost worked.

"What do you think of men who view their wives as property instead of a partner?"

Unlike her previous questions, this one he had no reservations about answering. "Men who hit are nothing more than cowards. Marriage isn't always easy, and sometimes it's really hard. A real man doesn't rely on fists or fear to get his way. He works together with his wife to find a solution to a problem."

As she considered his answer, Philip thought up a question about the first subject that popped into his mind—not from any real interest, but to steer Hannah away from further questions about himself.

"What's your aunt like?"

Hannah clasped her hands together and rested them beneath her chin. "I absolutely adore her. She's generous—whenever any of the neighbors have troubles she's the first to offer help. She's kind—all the children on her street love to sit in her kitchen or on her front porch because she always makes time to chat or play games. She's so many things—resourceful, a great cook, confident, and most of all, she's offering me and my son a new life."

Wanting to distract himself from the unexpected desire to learn more about a woman he'd never met, Philip began repacking his possibles bag. While he worked, Hannah rambled on about her aunt. He offered an occasional nod of his head or simple one-word replies, partially from the thrill of seeing her doing so much better now that her injuries had been tended to, and partially because it was a pleasure to hear stories of a woman who was opposite from his own wife in every way.

When his bag was tidied, closed, and the strap again rested against the right side of his neck and below his left arm, he finally asked the question he'd been pondering. "Do you think she'll ever find love again?"

"I think she gets lonely. She was so young when he died, and she's only thirty-nine years old. She's got plenty of life left to live." Hannah paused, considering her next words. "If she did ever decide to try again, the man would have to be loyal, brave yet gentle, and above all else, a believer."

****

Hours later, as they all relaxed by the fire under the moonlit sky, a sudden change about a mile away caught his eye.

Light!

Philip slowly set down the stick he'd been absently rolling one end of in the coals and straightened. Seconds later, the light faded, then went out.

"What is it?" Hannah craned her neck to allow her eyes to follow his distant stare.

Two sharp cracks sounded, then all went quiet.

"Did you hear that?" she asked, her whisper nearly as loud as Philip's heartbeat.

He silenced her with a grunt, then got to his feet,

pulling his knife from the sheath in his belt as he rose. With a series of hand motions, he instructed her to stay silent, stay put, and keep watch over Clark sleeping soundly at her side.

Wide-eyed, she nodded her understanding.

He crept off and spent the next two hours pacing an ever-widening circle around the camp, alert for signs of danger. He sighted nothing, and after the third hour he returned to where Hannah lay, awake and waiting.

"No problems," he said. "It was probably just one of the many animals that roam around these parts."

Hannah let out a long, trembling sigh. "Maybe a buffalo?"

"Could be," he agreed, even though he wasn't so certain. Especially given their decline over the recent years due to irresponsible and often wasteful hunting practices. All he knew for certain was the noises hadn't come from a gun. "Or it could have been another trapper. After all, I'm probably not the only man working this area. I'll keep watch all night, either here by the fire or out nearby, so don't worry if you wake and don't see me."

"What can I do?"

"Hannah, you need to sleep."

She answered his request by curling on her side and closing her eyes.

Chapter Twenty-Six
Third Day

Tuesday, December 21, 1886

Philip yawned and ran his hands over his eyes for the third time that morning. Though he wasn't a coffee drinker, after the night he'd had he could use a cup. Or five. At least his ceaseless patrolling of the area had found no cause for the noises they'd heard.

"Ready?" he asked, staring at the two who'd brought his long-dormant feeling of protectiveness flickering to life once again.

"Yes," Hannah said, hefting a now spry Clark in her arms. He'd woken in the middle of the night, nursed with a gusto that bordered on frantic, and immediately fallen asleep again. That morning he'd eaten again and was now bouncing in his mother's arms, much to her delight.

"He's feeling better, I see." Philip chuckled as he kicked dirt over last night's coals.

"That he is," Hannah said, giggling as her boy's mischievous left hand freed itself from its mitten and began tugging on her braid. His right arm remained bandaged to his chest, and he didn't seem to mind.

While Philip was thrilled to see the boy happy and alert, he worried of the toll it would take on Hannah. "Tonight I'll fashion together a papoose for him. Carrying him on your back will give your arms a rest, and he shouldn't mind the change because he'll still be close to you."

Hannah put her hand on his arm. "I didn't get a chance to say this last night, so I'll say it now—thank you for all you've done, and for all you're doing to help me and my son."

"You're welcome," Philip muttered gruffly, embarrassed at her praise.

They traveled the entire day without incident, but also without any food aside from weak pemmican broth and a tiny ration of jerky, nor any chance to refill his canteens. The snowfall from the other day had long since melted, leaving behind only wide stretches of muddy grass. They weren't due to meet up with a river until the end of the following day.

****

That night at the fire, while Clark nursed for the fifth

time that day, Philip used a length of twine to weave together three sides of two beaver pelts and then attached the crude sack to his stretching hoop. Shoulder straps consisted of two lengths of braided twine. His papoose would bring about scorn and ridicule from any squaw, but at least it was safe and sturdy. When he was done, he put everything away. Then, when camp was tidied and he had nothing left to distract himself, he sat and watched her across the flames.

"You warm enough?" She nodded, still as silent as she'd been while he'd fiddled with the papoose. "How about the boy? It's cold out tonight."

"We're fine." She adjusted the quilt around his head, then picked up his left hand and pressed it to her lips. The boy, content in his mother's arms and secure in her love for him, let out a sleepy string of babbles that lasted only a few minutes before his eyelids drooped and then slowly closed.

Hannah looked at Philip with a wry grin. "He's always fought me on going to sleep. Even when he was first born."

Philip chuckled softly, thinking of a little brown-eyed girl he'd once known who'd preferred sitting up in her cradle before the fire, watching everything go on around her instead of napping.

Eventually Hannah joined her son in slumber. Philip dozed for several hours until he saw a campfire flicker to life in the distance. He knew it wasn't a coincidence. Nor was it something he could ignore.

Someone was tracking them.

Chapter Twenty-Seven
Fourth Day

Wednesday, December 22, 1886

The first time Hannah tripped, Philip attributed it to a simple misstep. The second time, from a moccasin that had slipped off her foot. By the third time she went down he'd already faced the dim reality—she was struggling. Again. And this time, easy fixes like tending to her injuries and making a papoose weren't going to make a bit of difference. She needed food. They all did.

For what had to be the hundredth time that day, Philip wished he hadn't been so generous the first day they'd met. Now the jerky was gone and they'd eaten the last flakes of his pemmican as the previous day's midday meal. He'd thought he could make everything last until at least tomorrow night, but the dwindling supplies had been no match for their ravenous appetites.

Though he'd set a few snares each night in the hopes of catching small game, he'd collected only empty traps each morning. Hunting big game wasn't an option. He refused to risk leaving Hannah and Clark alone for hours, or possibly days, while he tracked antelope or deer.

Rest was another impossible luxury. Though he wanted to allow early nights and late departures, they all were teetering between hunger and starvation, weariness and exhaustion. It was vital to keep pushing on to their destination, which hopefully had a warm, well-stocked kitchen.

Philip helped Hannah to her feet, and while she brushed herself off he took a moment to surreptitiously inspect their back trail. For the fifth time that day he saw nothing.

Clark began fussing, and Hannah slipped the papoose straps from her shoulders. Philip helped her to the ground and then placed her son in her arms. She cradled him to her chest, but less than a minute later she looked at Philip with desperation in her eyes.

"He's still hungry, and I can't help him anymore."

Philip had known this moment would come, but had hoped it would be when they were only a few hours away from Great Falls. As she grew more worn down and malnourished, her supply would dwindle, leaving Clark's stomach to suffer. He dug inside his pack.

"Here," he said, filling a cup with precious water from his one of his canteens. They were due to hit water tomorrow; he could refill both then. "This will help."

"For a while anyway," she replied, cringing as the air filled with the boy's greedy slurps and grunts of satisfaction.

She was right. Filling the boy's stomach would leave him content for the night, and while water would prevent dehydration, it was no substitute for the nutrients he wasn't getting.

They were in a race against time and losing fast.

Chapter Twenty-Eight
Noise

Philip spent the latter half of the day walking shoulder to shoulder with Hannah, his arm twined in hers so she couldn't fall again. Pushing hard against the wind and the overwhelming desire to stop, they struggled on until the first star shone through the darkening sky and Great Falls was less than twenty miles away.

Philip led them into a hollow, and within minutes of easing Hannah to the ground, he had bedrolls spread and was on his knees, coaxing a fire to life. As the crackle of the first flames filled the air, so did another noise. A thump, soft but distinct.

"What was that?" Hannah asked, panic in her tone.

"Lay down," he muttered, getting to his feet and running a testing hand over his knife and revolver. "Stay here," he added, tossing the quilt over her and

Clark.

He scurried up to the rim of the hollow and dropped to his stomach several feet from the edge. The moonlight allowed him to see for miles and he scanned a rapid perimeter around the makeshift camp, familiarizing himself with the area.

His gut told him someone was close. Seconds later, his eyes confirmed it when he sighted a shadowy figure less than a quarter mile away and closing in fast. Looking back at where he'd left Hannah and Clark, Philip groaned when he saw the quilt in the firelight. A quilt that would be easily recognizable to its other owner. He thundered back down the hill and skidded to a stop beside Hannah.

"What is it?" she hissed.

"Someone's coming. The fire is too strong so there's no use trying to conceal the obvious that someone's down here. Best I can do is to try and make whoever it is out there believe it's just me in this camp." He wadded the quilt into a ball and shoved it beneath his supply pack. Then he lifted and lowered his own bedroll atop Hannah and Clark. "Stay hidden and do whatever you can to keep Clark quiet."

Positioning himself on the side of the hollow where he'd last seen the figure approaching, halfway between the rim and his fire, Philip waited.

Chapter Twenty-Nine
The Visitor

"That you, Philip?"

"Yes!" Philip grinned at the familiar voice of his friend, Emmett Fletcher. Once his heart and lungs calmed again, Philip climbed to the top of the hollow and shook the waiting man's outstretched hand.

"Good to see you again," Emmett said, clapping Philip on the shoulder. "It's been about a year, hasn't it?"

"About that," Philip agreed, grateful the unexpected guest was an old friend instead of a new foe.

Emmett eyed the knife still clutched in Philip's left hand. "You expecting trouble?"

"I've already found it," Philip replied, pointing to the motionless lump beside his fire.

Emmett's eyebrows rose in obvious curiosity. "What

you got down there?"

"See for yourself," Philip replied. After tucking his knife back into its sheath, he turned and led the way. Once they reached the bedroll, Philip leaned down and grabbed an edge.

"You got a new wife in there you don't want no one to see?" Emmett laughed, then quickly sobered as Philip straightened with the bedroll in his hands. Hannah and Clark lay still, blinking away discomfort at the sudden light across their faces.

Emmett let out a low whistle. "I'd say you found yourself a whole mess of trouble."

Philip tossed his bedroll aside, helped Hannah sit up, then lifted Clark and placed him in her arms. Once they were settled and he'd murmured assurances that this was a man he knew well and trusted, he rose and eyed Emmett.

"They got names?"

Philip nodded. "Emmett Fletcher, meet Hannah and Clark Dolt."

Emmett stepped toward Hannah, his hand outstretched in preparation for a shake, but he faltered when she leaned away from his reach. Straightening, he turned back to Philip. "I've traded in my furs at Fort Matiley and now I'm heading south. I can't help but wonder what you're doing?"

Philip opted to give the short version of the story.

"Taking these two to Great Falls."

Emmett eyed Philip's bundle of furs sitting beside the fire, but instead of questioning why he wasn't heading to the fort himself, he simply asked, "Mind if I sit for a while?"

After Philip gave a nod of permission, Emmett dropped his pack beside the fire, the resulting thump reminiscent of the noise they'd heard earlier. He put a hand on the small of his back as he stretched. "I'm getting too old to be lugging such a weight about the countryside."

"You and me both," Philip said, chuckling as they both let out their fair share of groans as they sank to the ground.

Emmett removed the leather bag slung over his shoulder, dug around inside, and removed a metal box and a pipe. After filling his pipe with fresh tobacco he lit it, took several puffs, and then leaned against his pack.

Conversation between the two men ensued, ranging from the weather to how each of them had fared during the trapping season. Then, when they'd both said all they had to say, Emmett shifted to give Philip a contemplative stare.

"You know there's a man on your back trail?"

"I had a hunch. He a trapper?" Philip asked, hopeful for an easy explanation for the noises and the far-off fires.

"Didn't strike me as such." Emmett tapped his ashes in the fire, then set his pipe aside. "I didn't much care for him, and I really didn't care for how he treated his dog."

"What did the dog look like?" Hannah asked, her voice wavering with fear.

"Big. All black except for a spot of white fur on his chest and the tip of one of his front paws." He looked to Hannah, regret shining strong in his eyes. "The man said he was looking for his wife and child. Said they'd gone missing a few days back, and he feared them lost."

Hannah gasped then went silent.

"Ma'am, you can tell a lot about a man by how he treats his animals. And judging by how his dog slunk around the camp, cringing at his every word, I'd say he wasn't the type to show a lick of kindness to his wife or child. I'd say they had good call to take off on him." He winked at Hannah. "In fact, if I were to run across him again, I'd be certain to point him in the opposite direction of what he's looking for."

"Thank you," she murmured.

Emmett's gaze went to the fire, empty of any pots or pans. "You finished dinner already?"

Philip shook his head. "Nope."

"'Bout to get started on making it then?"

"Fresh out of anything to make."

Emmett ran his hand along his jaw line several times, then motioned to Philip's pack while reaching for his own. "Give me your canteen."

"It's empty."

"I figured. Hand it over."

Philip obliged, then watched in disbelief as he spun open the lid of his own canteen and then poured the contents into Philip's.

"It's all I got," he said, shaking his canteen to allow the last few drops to trickle free.

"Better keep some for yourself, there's tough terrain—"

"I'll be fine," he replied, spinning both lids closed. "You've got bigger worries than looking for water."

After another glance at Hannah and Clark, he grimaced and dug into his pack again. "I almost forgot," he said, pulling out a lifeless ground squirrel and holding it aloft. "Looks like you could use this a sight better than I can right about now. Sorry it's not something more substantial, like an antelope, but it should be enough give you each a bite or two."

"Are you sure?" Philip asked, even as his mouth watered at the thought of freshly cooked meat.

"Yes," he replied, tossing it into Philip's outstretched hands. "I'm moving too fast to take the time to cook it, and I'd rather it go to three empty bellies than be torn to shreds by wild animals. Besides," he added, tipping his head toward Hannah and Clark, "seems like you all could stand to build up your strength for what's ahead."

He closed up his pack and then got to his feet. "I better be on my way."

"You can't stay for a late dinner?" Philip asked, also rising.

Emmett shook his head. "There's a special lady awaiting my presence down in Helena, and I don't aim to disappoint her." He turned to Hannah and gave her a jaunty tip of his hat. "Best wishes to you ma'am."

Though on the verge of tears, she smiled and murmured her goodbyes.

"I'll walk you out a ways," Philip said. Beckoning for Emmett to follow, he headed away from the fire.

"How bad is he?" Philip asked, once he was certain his words couldn't be overheard.

Emmett let out a long breath. "He's a mean one, seeking vengeance and following close. So close that he's already seen you with them. Told me he's biding his time, and when he's ready he'll get them back."

"I can't thank you enough for what you've done." Overwhelmed by his friend's generosity and how it would change their next few days of travel, Philip pulled him close and clapped him on the back several times before letting go. "Tight chains to you, Fletcher."

"Tight chains to you too," Emmett replied.

As he disappeared into the darkness, Philip considered how fortuitous it was to have run across a friend who was not only able to warn them of being followed, but also willing to provide them with enough food and water to keep them going. Maybe Hannah was right. Maybe someone was watching over them.

****

Upon his return to camp, he found Hannah eying him with dread. "I'm so sorry I've dragged you into such a mess. I truly didn't expect him to come after us."

Philip didn't have the heart to tell her a man who viewed his woman and child as property instead of something to cherish wasn't one to give up easily.

She cupped her chin in her palms, watching him intently. "What happens now?"

For the next few minutes Philip considered his answer as he prepared Emmett's gift for cooking. After dropping the meaty chunks into the pot, he set it in the flames. Pulling a serving spoon from his pack, he crouched near the fire and looked to Hannah.

"What happens now is we're going to have ourselves a nice dinner. Anything after that depends upon your husband."

Chapter Thirty
Stealthy Scouting

Philip kept watch on the rim of the hollow, and a few minutes past midnight a fire flickered to life about three miles to the north. He crept back to his own fire and knelt before Hannah.

"I'm going on a walk. I'll be back soon." It was long past time to see what he was up against.

"Don't!" She clutched his arm with surprising strength. "I know you're going after him. Don't."

He patted her hand in an effort to calm her. "I'm not going after him."

Her grip eased. "You're not?"

"No." *At least not tonight.* "He might be stronger than me, and he's definitely meaner." Philip grinned. "But I'm wiser, sneakier." *And sober.*

"If he catches you spying on him he'll hurt you!"

"Not if you give me the upper hand and tell me what

I need to know about him. What to watch out for."

Her fingers tapped her lips as she contemplated his request. "Our dog's name is Bruno. He loves Clark, and he's watched over him since the day Clark was born. As for William, he's short, but strong. Frightfully so. His preferred weapon is an ax; he's not good with a gun or a knife because they require steady aim, and he's usually drunk. I always worried he'd kill himself one day with a misplaced swing while working on our woodpile." She paused. "What else do you need?"

"Your sweater."

Without hesitation she took it off and handed it over. "Don't worry about me," he said, smoothly removing her hand from his arm and rising. "I'll be fine."

He left before she could convince him to stay. Rather, before he could convince himself to stay. After all, he was about to go up against a man much younger than himself. Even worse, the man had a dog. Tough to do battle against heightened hearing, scent, and sight.

He'd be stupid not to be afraid, but he'd be a coward if he stayed.

****

Fifty yards out, Philip could see the outline of a man sitting before his fire. Wild and wide arm gestures told of his anger, and the bottle making frequent visits to his lips confirmed his lack of character. The dog lay beside his master, gnawing on a stick.

Philip crept closer.

Twenty yards out, he saw William's hair was blond, his nose was thin, and his chin was weak. His coat fought to contain his lumberjack-sized shoulders and arms that rivaled tree trunks.

The man was a mess. Ranting about how he wouldn't stand for some old man taking care of his family, crying until his body shook with sobs, then boasting about getting his woman back and teaching her a lesson she'd remember the next time she thought about leaving him.

As Hannah had predicted, he had an ax. The blade looked freshly sharpened, the handle freshly painted, and it lay within easy reach. Philip shook his head in disgust; the man cared more for his ax than his own family. Finished scouting, he decided to head back to his camp. As he slowly rose, his right knee let out a pop that echoed like a gunshot.

William didn't notice, but the dog did. His head rose first, then his ears. Interest in the stick was quickly abandoned in favor of sniffing the air. Seconds later his lips curled back, exposing a long line of gleaming white teeth.

Philip kept still. The dog did not.

Rising to his feet, Bruno stared into the darkness about ten feet off from where Philip was hunkered in a half crouch. When he let out a long, low growl, Philip slowly spread Hannah's sweater over himself, hoping her scent would overpower his own.

William finally took note of his dog's behavior. "Who's there?" he shouted, the words garbled by hours of drink.

When no answer came, William gave the dog a half-hearted kick to the ribs. "Bruno, be quiet."

Though Philip had no ill will toward the animal, he was relieved to see William didn't trust in the wisdom and skill of his own dog. He slipped his hand into his pocket, fumbling for what he hoped was still there.

Meanwhile, Bruno slunk to other side of the fire. A gust of wind blew past Philip, bringing both his and Hannah's scent into William's camp. The dog's tail wagged, then seconds later he bared his teeth and let out another growl.

"Shut up!" William roared, rising to kick Bruno again.

Philip's palm closed around the pinecone he'd been searching for. With one smooth motion, he pulled it free and threw it high and far. It landed on the other side of William's camp, providing a distraction for Bruno and enough time for Philip to quietly scurry away.

Chapter Thirty-One
Fifth Day

Thursday, December 23, 1886

"Wake up, Hannah. We've got to go. Now."

Philip had spent all night creating a false trail for William to follow. While scuffing his feet so he'd leave long, fresh furrows in the dirt, he'd dragged one arm of her sweater along the ground for two miles in the wrong direction—east, then he'd circled back and done it again, this time heading south.

"Wake up," he repeated, kneeling to shake her shoulder. "We're getting close, less than twenty miles to go."

False dawn had finally arrived, and it was time for them to head west.

Considering all he'd seen last night, William had

likely drunk himself into oblivion. Philip figured a sluggish start, combined with the time wasted back-tracking the false trails, would put William behind by a few hours at minimum, or possibly even a day.

Hannah struggled to her feet and within minutes they were moving on again. Throughout the morning, the dreary sky and rising wind hinted at a looming storm. The temperature hovered just above freezing, and by early afternoon they'd seen both rain and snow. Thankfully, neither stayed long.

Arm in arm they trudged, heads bowed into the wind. Though frequent checks of their back trail revealed nothing followed, Philip kept pushing them on. With each passing hour Hannah's stride grew shorter, and by late afternoon her steps were only inches. Then suddenly, nothing.

"How's Clark doing?" Hannah asked, her voice so weak he had to strain to hear.

"He's sleeping. Are you ready to go again?" he asked, eager to roust her from her sudden stop. They'd only done about nine miles so far, and twilight was still hours away.

Her knees buckled and he slid his arm around her waist, holding her firmly against his side. If he let her fall again, he feared she might not get back up for several hours. By then, William could be closing in fast.

"Hannah, we have to go on. Let me carry Clark for

you." She was long past the point where a lighter load would give her time to build up her strength. If he didn't take Clark now, he'd end up carrying them both later.

"No." Her eyes fluttered closed. "I can take care of my son."

"I know you can," he said, slipping one of the papoose straps from her shoulder. "And you're doing a great job. Just let me take him."

Philip slid the other strap down her arm. Once the papoose was free he laid it upon his chest, stuck his arms through the straps, and then grabbed Hannah by the waist again.

"Are you a Godly man, Philip?" she asked, her tone a mixture of pleading and desperation.

He recalled the same question from days ago and his flippant answer. While he again found no reason to lie, he did consider his words more carefully.

"I've never thought of myself as such, but I'm not opposed to change either."

Chapter Thirty-Two
Sixth Day

Friday, December 24, 1886

Several days without substantial food had taken a hard toll on Philip. Though he had every intention of waking early and leaving fast, he simply couldn't force himself to rise. Not at false dawn, nor when the last star blinked from the sky. He lay still, resting. As did Hannah and Clark.

Only when the sun lingered over the horizon was Philip finally able to summon the strength to wake Hannah, get them both on their feet, and then load his body with his furs, supply pack, and Clark's papoose.

"Hannah, we've got less than ten miles to go. We can do this."

She gave him a weak nod and a weaker smile.

By the end of the first mile his left arm was wrapped around her waist, her right arm was draped around his shoulder, and her head hung low on her chest, bobbing with every step. Another mile in and his knees begged him to quit, and Hannah's incoherent babbling grew frightful, despondent.

"I'll never escape him," she moaned, dragging her feet to a stop and burying her forehead against his arm. "He'll find me. Hurt me. Hurt Clark. Hurt you."

"No, he won't. I won't let him." He said the words even though he barely had the strength to take another step, and his back felt as though it would splinter under the burden he bore. "We're almost there, Hannah. Nine miles at the most. Keep going, keep strong, and we'll be at your aunt's house tonight. Then you can celebrate Christmas together."

"I'm sorry," Hannah mumbled into his sleeve.

"You've got nothing to be sorry for." He patted her hand. "Try and take a few steps."

Hannah kept rambling. "I invited—no, dragged—you into my problems. Put you in danger..."

"I knew everything before I made my choice." Still patting her hand, he took a tentative step. She followed suit with one step, then another.

"My aunt's house sits on the Sun River. On the north side, just before it meets the Missouri. It's a small, white house. A split-rail fence runs along the left side of the property, and there's a forked oak tree in the front yard."

Philip nodded, more to encourage her to keep walking than from interest of what he'd heard. "You're doing great. Let's see if you can go a little faster."

"I can't," she cried, pulling him to a stop. "I can't!"

He spun her to face him. "Yes you can. Yes you will. For your son."

She burst into tears. "I don't think God cares about me anymore."

"Don't say that!" His tone was fierce. "Look at all the things he's done for you so far. How he's protected you. He put me on the path to find you. Helped me make the right choice. He sent Emmett Fletcher to warn us, and to give us food and water. He's been there for you every step of the way." Holding her by the shoulders, he looked deep in her eyes. "Hannah, he's here with you now. And so am I. Try one more step?"

"Please," she whispered. "Save my son."

Seconds later, her eyes rolled back in her head and she went limp in his arms.

Chapter Thirty-Three
Discarding the Obvious

Hannah was alive, but barely. Same for Clark. They both needed help, fast. But first he had to find a way to get rid of his furs and supply pack so William wouldn't spot them, providing an instant confirmation he was on the right trail.

Burning them would give away their location. Burying them wouldn't work either. The amount of dirt disturbed would be huge and even if William didn't notice it, his dog would.

Philip spun in a circle, frantic to discover any way to leave them behind. Sighting a collection of jagged boulders in the distance, he started walking. Ten minutes later he was a hundred pounds lighter and heading back to Hannah's side. She lay exactly how he'd left her, except now she shivered from the cold.

"I'm here," he said, figuring his voice might provide her comfort. Besides, if she could still hear him, she might eventually answer. "I'm moving Clark, and then we'll be on our way."

After he repositioned the papoose and his possibles bag to his back and the quilt around Hannah, he knelt beside her. He eased his right arm below her knees and his left around her back. With a long grunt, he straightened.

Arms and lungs burning with exertion, Philip headed east. After three jolting steps, her eyes fluttered open and she murmured the now-familiar question, "Are you a Godly man, Philip?"

Five steps later he gave his answer. "I'm trying."

Chapter Thirty-Four
Trickery

The barking was unmistakable. Given the clarity, the dog was less than a mile away.

Philip glanced at the trees lining the Sun River, and figured one of them would be the perfect spot to stash Hannah and Clark while he lured William into the open. Since discovery was inevitable, he might as well get the upper hand.

Hannah woke with a groan while he was struggling to prop her against a tree. "What's happening?" she murmured, rolling her head from side to side.

"William's close," he said, placing her son in her arms. "Clark's sleeping, but if he wakes you need to keep him quiet."

She sat up, blinking the confusion from her eyes. "William's here?"

"Not yet." He slid his right hand against her back, tipped her forward, and used his left hand to tug her quilt free. "I need this."

Fear snapped her into full alert and she grabbed his wrist. "Where are you going?"

"To find your husband before he finds you." He yanked off his possibles bag, tossed it beside her, and then pressed his revolver into her hand. "Ever used one before?"

"No," she said, watching him slowly rise. "What can I do to help?"

Philip's heart raced as two quick barks and then a shout echoed across the land. "Pray."

Quilt in one hand and knife in the other, he turned and ran toward what he'd just heard. He made it twenty yards before Bruno appeared at the crest of the next hill. Alone. Ceaseless barking let Philip know he'd been sighted, and he quickly dropped to the ground and covered himself with the quilt.

Chapter Thirty-Five
Confrontation

Philip's hands kept desperate hold as the dog's paws and snout explored the quilt. Seconds later, he heard approaching footsteps and a man's voice repeating Hannah's name in gruff singsong. Then the steps stopped.

Philip stayed silent, motionless, even as either a boot heel or ax handle poked him from head to toe.

"Time to quit hiding, Hannah." William kicked Philip in the gut.

Unwilling to give up the ruse yet, Philip held back a grunt.

"That old man left you, didn't he?" Footsteps again, then a rustle of grass. Warm, rancid air against Philip's cheek let him know William was now crouched beside his head. "Even a coot like him could see you're worthless."

Surprise on his side, Philip flung the quilt wide and came up swinging. He landed two fast punches—jaw and gut—then took a step back, shaking his hand. The man was so solid it was like punching a bear.

"Cowards throw sucker punches," William groused, holding his jaw and glaring at Philip.

Philip's eyebrows rose. "Cowards hit women."

William snorted. "Hannah's *my* wife, and I'll teach her how I see fit."

Philip stepped in for another swing, but William's reflexes were faster. He ducked the punch and wrenched the knife from Philip's hand.

"I was gonna go easy on you." William's lips twisted into a humorless grin. "Not now."

Philip was down on the ground before he even knew he'd been hit.

"Where's my wife?" William asked, tossing the knife aside. It landed next to his ax lying in the grass.

"Far away," Philip sputtered through the bloody froth filling his mouth. "You'll never hurt her again."

"You'll tell me." Lightning fast, William punched his ear. "Eventually. In the meantime, we'll have ourselves a good fight." William hovered over him, cracking his knuckles one by one. "Where's my wife?"

Philip shook his head, his stomach roiling as stars littered his vision.

A soft voice startled them both. "I'm right here."

Philip groaned to see Hannah standing less than ten yards away, Clark in her arm, Bruno by her side, and his revolver nowhere in sight.

Sighting his wife, William's eyes narrowed. "I've seen you with this man." He pointed at Philip, now on his hands and knees and trying to rise. "How could you let him touch you? Touch our son?"

"He tended the aftermath of your last beating. Nothing more." Hannah met his glare with her own. "I'm not going back with you, William."

He scoffed. "I don't want you back. All I ever wanted from you was to clean my house, cook my food, and warm my bed. You're horrible at all three."

"Then why did you follow me? Why not let me go?"

William paused, contemplating his answer, and Philip saw his chance.

"Hannah, run!" he shouted, then sprang through the air. He landed with his arms wrapped around William's knees, and drove his weight forward. William's torso landed first, his head slammed to the ground seconds later. With a strength fueled by anger, Philip scrambled across the dirt and sat hard on William's chest, trapping the man's arms at his sides. His first punch landed true, and he felt William's nose give way beneath his fist.

The telltale click of a gun's hammer settling into

place stopped them both.

"Leave him alone." Hannah's command was firm, fierce, and for a sickening moment Philip wasn't certain at who her words were directed. His gaze went from her to the man on the ground beneath him, his arms curled protectively around his head. What had he become?

Seconds later, Philip saw the barrel of his gun rise, then level off at William's chest. "Leave us all alone."

William's arms lowered. He sighted the gun in Hannah's hand and stared at her in astonishment. "Well, look who got brave."

Hannah's aim never wavered. "William, get up."

"Gladly," William replied, heaving Philip aside and then scrambling to his feet.

"Now go!" she shouted.

William wiped blood from his upper lip with his coat sleeve, then shook his head. "Not without you. Not without my son."

Hannah kissed Clark on the forehead, then slid her index finger from the side of the gun to the trigger.

"Hannah, don't." Fighting through the pain, Philip got to his feet. "Don't do something you'll regret for the rest of your life."

"I have to," Hannah pleaded, her eyes locking with Philip's. "Don't you understand? He'll never stop hurting me, or hunting me."

Hands outstretched with the intent to take over her burden, Philip took a step forward. His vision blurred and he felt his knees give out. As he tried to regain his balance he heard Hannah's gut-wrenching scream.

"William, no!"

Philip turned, but it was too late. William rammed the end of his ax handle into Philip's stomach, sending him flying. Gasping for breath, Philip lay sprawled on the ground, powerless to do anything as William dropped the ax and headed for Hannah.

Squeezing her eyes shut, she pulled the trigger.

Though the bullet tore a bloody furrow along his forearm, rage made him fearless. He charged her, twisted the gun from her hand, and hurtled it through the air. After watching it land far from anyone's reach, he glared at Hannah.

"You aren't fit to raise my son!" William wrenched Clark free from her grip and shoved her until she fell. Tucking the boy under his arm, he turned toward the hill he'd come from. Two steps in, Clark wriggled free from his father's hold and fell to the ground, headfirst.

William whirled and stared at Hannah, his mouth agape. "Look what you made me do!"

"It's not my fault!" she screamed, scurrying across the dirt toward her motionless son. "You're the one who grabbed him! Dropped him!"

"You did this," he roared. "You left me." His fist

caught her just under her chin and her head twisted to the side. Her body landed beside Clark's with a lifeless thud.

"Hannah!" Philip crawled to her side and patted her cheek. "Hannah?"

William's face went bone-white, his eyes wide with horror. "Are they...?"

Philip eased open one of her eyelids and studied her eye for several moments, then did the same with Clark. After he saw what he needed, he glared at William while shrugging free from his coat. "You've finally done what you've tried to do for years. You've killed her! Your son too!"

Tears streaming down his cheeks, William took a step closer. "I never meant to..."

"Go!" Philip yelled, covering Clark's body and Hannah's face with his coat. "You've done what you came here to do, so just go."

Without another word, William spun around and ran back over the hillside.

Chapter Thirty-Six
Seeking Guidance

Bruno stood beside Philip, whining and nudging Clark's hand with his snout.

"Just a few more minutes," Philip said, his eyes scanning the horizon for any sign of movement. Only when he was certain William wasn't coming back did he dare to lift his coat.

He'd lied. Hannah and Clark were alive.

However, the situation was grave. Clark was alert and trying to sit up, but he'd taken a hard hit to the head. Philip couldn't rouse Hannah no matter how hard he tried. Clutching his stomach, he slowly got to his feet, pausing several times to catch his breath. Once he was standing and certain he'd stay that way, he glanced at Bruno, now stretched out along Clark's side. Could he trust a dog he didn't know?

"Bruno," he said, taking care to keep his tone friendly.

The dog's tail thumped once in reply, then went still.

Philip extended his hand, palm out. "Bruno, stay."

The dog stared at him, then gave Clark's forehead a soft lick.

Bruno didn't move when Philip took his first of many hesitant steps to where he'd seen his revolver and knife land. Nor did he follow when Philip shuffled by again, this time on his way to retrieve his possibles bag and Clark's papoose.

When he returned, he knelt beside Clark. Under Bruno's watchful brown eyes, he coaxed the boy into the papoose. Once the straps were in place and Clark was again settled safely on his back, Philip looked to Hannah.

She hadn't moved.

For the past day he'd used the Sun River as his guide, knowing it would eventually lead him directly into Great Falls. Trouble was, the river took its time getting there—a meandering route that featured many switchbacks. As the crow flew, Hannah's aunt's house was less than three miles away. Following the river, it was about six. Abandoning the certainty the river provided would save time—something he couldn't spare right now, given Hannah and Clark's condition—but he wasn't too familiar with the area and worried of becoming lost.

Distance versus certainty, a monumental decision.

Philip closed his eyes against the sting of looming tears, and, for the first time in eighteen years, he prayed.

"God, I need your help. I need you to show me the path to take, so I can get Hannah and her boy to safety." He choked back a sob. "And I need you to give me the strength to get them there. I'm hurting bad, and if I can't make it, they'll die out here. Please, help me?"

Philip felt something warm and soft slide across his cheek and opened his eyes to see Bruno beside him, licking away his tears. Patting the dog on the head, he rose and went to Hannah. After several deep breaths, he bent and gathered her in his arms. Rising again, he took a few steps. To his surprise, he found his balance intact and his strength sure.

With Bruno trotting along at his heel, Philip started walking.

Chapter Thirty-Seven
Paulina

The house was just as Hannah had described, down to the fence and the fork in the tree. On the verge of collapse, he lumbered down the stone walkway, up two steps, and onto the porch. Two rocking chairs swayed gently from the motion of his labored footsteps as he crossed the weathered wood floor.

"We're here, Hannah," he murmured, propping his shoulder against the wall and then rapping his knuckles against the door. Over the past hour he'd been able to rouse her twice, and he'd counted at least ten whimpers of protest from Clark. Though his noises were woeful, Philip was thrilled to hear anything from him at all.

"Hello?" he shouted, knocking again. "I need help!"
Still no answer.

Someone was home. Or at least close by. He'd spotted smoke drifting from the chimney when he was still a quarter-mile from the house. Well, he wasn't about to wait any longer to get Hannah and Clark the care they needed, and he wasn't about to lay them out on a cold porch when warmth—and by the smell of things, freshly baked bread—was so close.

Summoning what little of his strength remained, Philip nudged Bruno out of his way, centered himself in the doorway and began kicking in the door.

Three tries in the door swung wide, not because of his effort, but because of the petite woman who finally pulled it open. Her blue eyes widened to see what waited on her porch, but to her credit she didn't scream.

"It's your niece. Hannah. And her son."

She gasped, put one hand over her heart, and beckoned him inside with the other. "There's a bedroom in the back. I'll lead the way."

He stepped in, but didn't follow. "Ma'am?"

"Yes?" she asked, turning so fast her blond braid swung through the air.

"A table will work best to start."

"Of course," she said with an efficient nod. "Kitchen's to the left." Rushing ahead, she cleared a sugar bowl, glass pitcher, and butter dish off the table, then stepped back as he carefully lowered Hannah onto it. His heart soared with joy to hear her groans of protest as he worked to lay her flat.

"Hannah," he said, clutching his own stomach and leaning in close. "We're at your aunt's house. I'm going to check over Clark first, and then we're going to help you."

"What can I do?" the aunt asked after he'd straightened again.

"Help me get her boy off my back." He turned, showing her the crude papoose. "I can't trust my arms, and fear I'll drop him."

Under his direction, she removed the papoose, laid it on the floor, and then slowly removed Clark, who was alert, but teary-eyed.

"He took a bad fall a few hours ago. I'd like you to hold him while I check him over," Philip instructed, already feeling beneath the boy's coat to check on his arm. The bandage had held. Next, he eyed the knot on the center of his forehead, then ultimately decided it was something to watch, but not life-threatening.

"Do you have a cow?" he asked.

She nodded.

"Good. We'll give him some milk after we look over Hannah. He's too weak to be a nuisance, so for now we'll just set him on the floor while we work." While the aunt settled Clark on a blanket, Philip slid his possibles bag from his shoulder, then grimaced as bursts of pain rippled across his stomach.

She gave him a questioning look. "Do you need to sit?"

"No. Let's get started." He dropped the bag on the corner of the table and braced his hands on the edge. "I'm worried about her jaw. Let's hope it's not broken."

They worked side by side, treating Hannah's wounds—both old and new. Her jaw wasn't broken, but would be sore for weeks to come. As would her ribs. They placed new bandages and fresh salve on her temple, cheek, and foot. Throughout it all her eyes never opened, but after Philip carried her into one of the bedrooms and placed her on the mahogany four-poster bed, she managed a weak smile.

"Hannah, you're safe now, and so is your son." He ran his palm over her forehead, wishing something so simple could soothe away the troubles that weren't even beginning to plague her yet. "Your aunt and I want you to rest, but before you do I want you to know I'm really proud of you."

Eyes still closed, she murmured, "Her name is Paulina."

He chuckled, then looked at the woman watching him from the other side of the bed. "Nice to meet you, Paulina."

Paulina raised her eyebrows and gave him a gentle smile. "And what shall I call you?"

"Philip," he replied, smiling in return.

Chapter Thirty-Eight
Questions

Hours later, Philip woke to a lovely sight—Paulina standing before him, a tray of food in her hands. His stomach grumbled to see a bowl of hearty vegetable soup, a slice of bread slathered with butter, a cup of milk, and a tall glass of water.

"Everything looks great," he said, running his fingers through his hair and beard in a futile attempt to smooth everything into place. To his embarrassment, he'd fallen asleep on her settee in front of the fireplace.

"I figured I'd start with something light." She set the tray on a nearby table. "I've got more satisfying meals planned for later in the week, once you feel up to eating."

"First I have to check on Hannah and Clark." Though he gritted his teeth and pressed his palm over his stomach, he still grunted as he started to rise.

"Don't get up," she said, placing a firm hand on his arm. "They're fine."

With another unbecoming grunt, he relaxed again.

Paulina's hand dropped to her side. "She woke about an hour ago, and I gave her half a glass of water and two spoonfuls of chicken broth. Clark's doing remarkably better, so I fed him half a bowl of oatmeal thinned with milk. The dog ate the rest, then gobbled down a few scraps and a piece of bread. All three of them are now fast asleep." Her lips stretched into an adorable smile as she waved a finger at him. "As you will soon be too, after you eat everything on this tray."

"Yes ma'am," he said, grinning while giving her a mock salute. Then, he proceeded to do exactly as ordered.

****

Late in the evening, Philip's appetite returned and he ate everything Paulina set before him. Then, after she began washing the dishes without his help—he'd asked and she'd refused—he went back to the front room and eased himself down onto the settee. And then promptly stood again, realizing he was soiling the fabric with his filthy clothes and the room with his stench.

He headed for the kitchen. "Paulina?"

She turned. "Yes?"

"I hate to bother you for anything else, but could I

make use of a bucket of water? I had to leave behind my supply pack and frankly, I'm a mess."

She waved a sudsy hand through the air, dismissing his concern. "You're fine. However, I do have water heating on the stove and a small washtub out back. I hope you don't think it too presumptuous of me, but I also put out soap, a washrag, and a set of clean clothes that should fit you. Go on and handle your business, and afterward we'll sit in the front room with some raspberry tea and have ourselves a nice chat."

Looping his possibles bag over one hand and holding the handle of a pot of steaming water with the other, he headed past the bedroom where Hannah, Clark, and Bruno were sleeping and stepped onto the screened-in back porch. Paulina followed him, carrying two additional buckets of water, one warm and one cold.

"The three of these should combine to give you the perfect temperature." She set them on the floor beside the tub, straightened, and looked him over, head to toe. "Drop what you're wearing now in the water when you're done. They can soak overnight. I'll see you inside when you're finished."

Philip watched her leave, appreciating the view as she walked away. Now there was a woman worth washing up for!

Upon his return, he found Paulina sitting in a chair

beside the fireplace. A mug of tea and slice of apple pie waited for him on the side table beside the settee.

Philip knew what was coming. A woman could only wait so long before needing to pry. After the shock of what she'd found at her doorstep that morning, he figured she'd have plenty of questions.

"How did you two meet?" she asked. "You a neighbor of hers?"

At least she'd let him finish his pie first, though he'd barely gotten the plate back to the table before she fired off the first inquiry.

"Not a neighbor. I'm a fur trapper who happened upon her and the boy in the woods. She'd left her home a day earlier."

"Did her husband do that to you?" She motioned to his face.

"Yes," he replied, running his hand over his still-tender ear. "Though I did manage to give him some lasting reminders of myself too."

"Where's he at now?"

"William? I suspect he's about halfway home, sitting in front of a fire, drinking away his sorrows. Either way, after how we left things I don't expect Hannah and the boy will have trouble from him again."

She grimaced. "I knew from the minute I met him he was a horrible man."

Philip scoffed. "He doesn't deserve to be called a

man. He's a monster. That poor girl has been through more horrors than men twice her age."

"Given all my sister—Hannah's mother—had told me, I thought she was happily married. I had no idea of her suffering. Then last month I found two letters she'd written to her parents. I cried over every word." Paulina lowered her gaze to the floor. "Even now, I can't stop thinking of how scared and confused she must of have been the night she was forced to leave their home." A sob caught in her throat and she pressed her hand to her mouth. "Or how she felt that because of an argument we'd had the week before, that she couldn't come to me for help."

Philip started to rise, then hesitated. While he wanted to succumb to the overwhelming urge to comfort this woman, he wasn't sure if offering her a shoulder to cry on was too forward considering how they'd just met that morning. He settled instead for reassuring her of all she'd done right.

"Hannah speaks very highly of you, and of times you shared while she was growing up." He thought for a moment, then added, "She and Clark are fortunate to have a woman like you in their lives."

"I sent out a letter to her right away, urging her to come live here with me. I had no idea she'd be here so soon. I can't imagine what she was thinking, leaving in the middle of winter. Trying to travel so far on her own."

Philip frowned. "I'll leave it up to her to tell you the details, but in the end, she couldn't risk staying even one more day."

Paulina gave him a contemplating look. "What about you? What did you risk—or sacrifice—to bring her here?"

He let out a long sigh, trying to release some of the strain and worry that had dominated his world for the past week. "There's a year's worth of furs sitting a few miles away from here. I couldn't carry them and Hannah, so I left them. I knew she'd barely make it to Great Falls *with* my help, but I knew she and the boy would die if I refused." He shrugged and gave her a rueful grin. "An easy choice."

"Now that you've succeeded, why not plan to retrieve your furs?"

"To be honest, I hadn't really considered the idea. Until now." Stroking his bare jaw, he stared at Paulina with rising admiration for her practicality. She was right. He'd hidden the bundle in a spot well protected from snow. Since they were dried, he could leave them for a while, months even. He'd just have to fetch them before the hard rains of spring.

Paulina rose and took his empty plate and mug to the kitchen. When she returned, she carried two mugs in one hand and a wicker basket in the other.

"Let me help you," he said, rising to relieve her of the mugs. He waited until she'd sat in her chair again, then set her mug within reach on the nearby table. He returned to the settee with the other mug, then watched her unpack a needle, thread, and scissors from the basket. After she'd threaded the needle and made a few stitches in what appeared to be a child's quilt, she looked at him with apology in her eyes.

"I hope you don't think me rude, but I need to finish this tonight. It's a present for an expectant young couple from my church." She bowed her head. "I find winter nights tend to be long and lonely, so I've taken up sewing quilts as a way to pass the time."

Philip leaned down to where he'd left his possibles bag, reached inside, and pulled out his powder horn. Holding it aloft, he turned it slowly so she could see the elaborate carvings covering every inch. "I understand loneliness."

Her gaze grew hopeful. "Are you a Godly man?"

His lips parted in surprise at the familiar question. "Your niece asked me that several times on the way here."

Paulina's soft, lilting laugh washed over him, filling him with a happiness he hadn't felt in a long time. "From a young age, Hannah understood the importance of God in a person's life. When she grew older, she talked often of my remarrying after my husband died, and making sure that the person I chose was a believer."

"She's a smart girl." Philip set the horn on the table, wanting her to have his undivided attention. "As to your earlier question, I'll say that I was once, long ago." He let out a shaky breath and gave her a shy smile. "And thanks to Hannah, I am again now."

Chapter Thirty-Nine
Christmas Day

Saturday, December 25, 1886

Philip spent the morning eating good food cooked by a good woman, and helping entertain Clark and Bruno so Hannah could continue to rest. By late in the afternoon Hannah was awake, alert, and asking to see her son. After a quick discussion, Philip and Paulina decided to oblige her wishes. Philip carried Clark into the room, and Paulina followed with yet another bowl of chicken broth.

"Merry Christmas, everyone," Hannah murmured, her eyes shining with joy as they surrounded her bed.

"Merry Christmas to you," he replied, shifting Clark in his arms so she could see him easier. While he wasn't fully recovered, he was starting to show interest in holding his green cloth and playing with Bruno's tail, which was encouraging. "How are you feeling?"

"Better." She gasped. "You don't have a beard! You don't look so—"

"Grizzled?" he finished, then laughed at the crimson stain spreading across her cheeks.

With a mischievous glint in her eye, she beckoned him closer. "You told me the first thing you'd do when you found a woman you wanted to impress was shave off your beard."

He winked at her, then straightened.

Hannah gave him a chiding smile. "All this time I thought you regretted stumbling upon my quilt that day."

Philip had spent the past eighteen years living as a recluse, believing he had nothing to count on except his inevitable death. Now that he'd learned to trust in God again he realized his life was far from over. In fact, it was just beginning.

Smiling broadly, he looked across the room at Paulina. "Actually, I think it's one of the best things that's ever happened to me."

Apple Pie Recipe

I found this recipe imprinted on the bottom of a vintage pie plate. I've used it countless times and my family really enjoys the flavors. (My tip: cut each tablespoon of butter into four square pieces and place all eight pieces evenly across the apples)

1. Line pie pan with pastry.
2. Fill with 6 cups pared, sliced, tart apples.
3. In a bowl combine ¾ cup sugar, one tablespoon cornstarch, and one teaspoon cinnamon.
4. Sprinkle over apples. Dot with two tablespoons butter.
5. Cover with slit pastry. Seal edges.
6. Bake at 400 degrees for 45 to 60 minutes.

Other Books by Christi Corbett

ALONG THE WAY HOME

They lost everything but their dreams on the Oregon Trail...

Kate Davis is intrigued when her father reveals his dream of starting a horse ranch in Oregon Territory. Settlers out west value a strong woman, and though she manages the financials of her father's mercantile her competence earns her ridicule, not respect, from Virginia's elite society.

Jake Fitzpatrick, an experienced trail guide, wants land out west to raise cattle and crops. But dreams require money and he's eating dandelion greens for dinner. So when a wealthy businessman offers double wages to guide his family across the Oregon Trail, Jake accepts with one stipulation--he is in complete control.

Departure day finds Kate clinging to her possessions as Jake demands she abandon all he deems frivolous, including her deceased mother's heirlooms. Jake stands firm, refusing to let the whims of a headstrong woman jeopardize the wages he so desperately needs--even a beautiful one with fiery green eyes and a temper to match.

Trail life is a battle of wills between them until tragedy strikes, leaving Jake with an honor-bound promise to protect her from harm and Kate with a monumental choice--go back to everything she's ever known or toward everything she's ever wanted?

TAINTED DREAMS

Sometimes, the end justifies the means...

Kate Davis arrived into Oregon City transformed from a pampered daughter of fortune into a determined woman with a plan--fulfill her father's dream of starting a horse ranch in Oregon Territory.

She quickly discovers a harsh truth--even thousands of miles from home, on an unsettled land America doesn't yet own or govern, gender still takes precedence over ability. Refusing to be ruled once again by the stifling laws and societal norms she'd escaped by leaving Virginia, Kate begins creatively claiming what is rightfully hers.

Until a visit to the land office changes everything.

Jake Fitzpatrick guided Kate across the Oregon Trail, and fell in love with her along the way. Now he wants to marry her and build a life together, but a ruthless man from Jake's past threatens to reveal a dark secret, and destroy everything he's worked so hard to achieve.

Praise for *Along the Way Home*

In *Along the Way Home*, author Christi Corbett unfurls an unforgettable epic romance inside of an epic Western adventure. Beautifully crafted, this debut novel is a tender journey of the heart as well as a treacherous journey of many miles. *Along the Way Home* is a squeaky-clean historical romance with authentic period details and deep emotion. Much danger, risk, courage and compassion will make you long for more books from this talented author. As heartwarming as *Christy*."

—Eve Paludan,
author of the *Ranch Lovers Romance* series

****

A breathtaking account of courage and adventure along the Oregon Trail. Travel this dangerous journey with characters you will treasure as they cope with heart-wrenching difficulties they never thought to encounter in a search to fulfill their hopes and dreams. Christi Corbett's debut novel, *Along the Way Home*, will both surprise and delight.

—Jillian Kent,
author of *The Ravensmoore Chronicles*.

****

A dash of action! A touch of intrigue! Loads of sweet, clean romantic promise...

—Reid Lance Rosenthal,
Winner of 15 National Awards, #1 Best Selling Author of the *Threads West, An American Saga* series.

About the Author

Christi Corbett, winner of the 2013 RONE Award for Best American Historical novel and the 2014 Laramie Award (First in Category for Pioneer/Prairie fiction), lives in a small town in Oregon with her husband and their twin children. The home's location holds a special place in her writing life; it stands just six hundred feet from the original Applegate Trail and the view from her back door is a hill travelers looked upon years ago as they explored the Oregon Territory and beyond.